For Man

MW00978843

A different view of
life in the country!

Love,

Jen.

COUNTRY LIVING

JEN SILVER

COUNTRY LIVING

JEN SILVER

Affinity
Rainbow Publications

2020

Country Living
© 2020 by Jen Silver

Affinity E-Book Press NZ LTD
Canterbury, New Zealand

1st Edition

ISBN: 978-1-98-858849-0

Editor: CK King
Proof Editor: Alexis Smith
Cover Design: Irish Dragon Design
Production Design: Affinity Publication Services

ACKNOWLEDGMENTS

A big thank you, as always, to the publishing team at Affinity Rainbow Publications. Their continued support and belief in my ability as a writer has kept me going on my writing journey.

Thanks also to my wife, Anne, for her unwavering love and encouragement, enabling me to follow my dreams.

(Note: Although I did obtain professional advice on sheep farming and other agricultural pursuits, any misrepresentation of these activities is entirely down to me.)

DEDICATION

To the beauty of the countryside in the part of West Yorkshire where this story is set - country living at its best.

TABLE OF CONTENTS

PART ONE

Jen Silver

CHAPTER ONE

Their destination came into view as they reached the top of the narrow lane. Peri sighed in contentment. Moving-in day had finally come; the converted shepherd's croft was her dream cottage. Life might begin at forty for some, but Peri's new life was starting at sixty.

Glancing at her wife, Peri could see no signs of enthusiasm as Karla parked the Range Rover near the front door. Perhaps she was just tired from the long drive. Not surprising with their early start.

They'd set off from their home in Putney at daybreak. At least the four-and-a-half-hour drive from South London to this part of West Yorkshire had been fairly stress free at that time of day. They only made one brief stop at a service station near Nottingham.

Karla's silence had seemed to deepen the closer they got to the cottage. *Maybe I should have taken up Dana's offer to make the journey with me.* There would have been no shortage of conversation with her best friend. Although Peri was looking forward to the move, she knew she would miss the weekly coffee sessions when they would meet up to put the world to rights.

Peri climbed out of the car and gave her legs a shake, stiff from sitting so long. She found the key lock case by the kitchen window and gained access with the code she'd been sent on completion of the sale. Taking out the key, she used it to open the front door. With only a quick glance at the kitchen, Peri moved through to the living room that opened onto a patio.

A stunning view across a tree-lined valley gave no hint of the busy road below. Peri threw open the patio doors and took in a deep breath of fresh air.

"Isn't it just simply gorgeous, K?"

Karla grunted as she dropped two large suitcases by the sofa. "Yeah. Nice. Grab a box. Let's get everything in before the rain starts again."

Emptying the boot of the Range Rover didn't take long. The large vehicle looked out of place on city streets but would be perfect when Karla finally joined her at the cottage. Six months wasn't too long to wait for her wife to finish the various projects she was working on. Then they could start this new phase of their life together.

The rain started again, as predicted, just as Karla carried the last box inside.

"The water's running okay. I'll put the kettle on when I find it," Peri called out from the kitchen.

Karla leaned against the doorway and brushed a strand of her long dark hair away from her face. "I won't stay for coffee. I'll just use the loo and head back."

"Seriously, K? You need a rest after that drive."

Finding the kettle was easy. She'd labelled the boxes herself and made sure one with the kitchen supplies was the first box carried into the cottage. Karla relented when Peri handed her a mug after she emerged from the bathroom.

Peri led the way into the living room and stood by the patio doors again. "Look, a rainbow." The rain had stopped, and the brightly coloured arch spanned the gap between the valley tops.

Karla stood next to her, gulping her coffee. "Mm. Nice."

Not sure whether her wife meant the view or the drink, Peri wrapped her arm around Karla's waist. "It's a sign. We're going to be so happy here."

Anything Karla might have added was cut off by her phone's ringtone. "That'll be Aldo. I'd better take it." She pulled the device out of her back pocket in one swift move and walked back into the kitchen.

It wasn't unusual for Karla's boss to call her on a Sunday. As a senior manager with the international IT company, when Aldo Templeton called, Karla responded. Peri was used to the lack of set working hours and days, but she would be glad when they could both be settled in the country.

"I really have to go now. You'll be okay with all this, won't you?" Karla returned from the kitchen and waved her hands in the direction of the boxes piled up in front of the fireplace.

"Of course." Peri reached up and stroked her face. "Drive carefully and call me when you get home."

"I always drive carefully."

"Says she with six points on her licence."

"They come off next April, so I'll be fine."

After extracting a promise that Karla would stop at a service station before she got too tired, Peri waved her off and went back inside to survey her new domain.

The furniture left by the owners was adequate for her needs. The sofa and accompanying armchair both looked a bit lumpy, but they would do until Karla was ready to move. Then they'd sell the London house and furnish the cottage properly. Peri looked forward to having her favourite recliner there.

With another mug of coffee in hand, she wandered over to the patio doors to check out the state of the garden. Even through the rain sheeting across the valley, she could visualise the potential. In preparation for the change in her lifestyle, Peri had taken a practical gardening course over the winter months and stocked up on back issues of *Homes and Gardens*.

Giving herself a mental shake, Peri put her mug down on the window ledge and gazed back into the room. What to do first? Kitchen, bedroom, set up laptop. If only Karla could have stayed to give her a hand. Peri had known in advance that wouldn't happen. She would have to settle for Karla's weekend visits for the near future.

Best to get connected to the world. Peri had marked out the alcove at the side of the fireplace for her work area. There was a handy telephone point and convenient sockets. Amazingly, everything worked at the first attempt. The strength of the signal was as advertised and would make her plan of working from the cottage entirely feasible. Smiling at the success of the installation, she picked up her phone and sent Karla a message to let her know.

There was a text from her best friend, Dana, checking to see if they'd made it. Peri sent her a smiley emoji. Seconds later, her phone rang with Dana's face lighting up the screen.

"So, all good?"

"You bet. It's raining at the moment, but I know it's going to be fantastic."

"Is Karla helping you settle in?"

"No, she had to go straight back."

"Shit. I should have come with you. Will you be okay on your own?"

"Of course. I've got loads to do to make it shipshape."

"I can't believe she didn't stay at least for your first night."

"Honestly, it's not a problem. This place has a great vibe. I'll be fine."

"Well, you certainly picked the right part of the country to settle in. Hebden Bridge is touted as the lesbian capital of the north."

"The cottage is a few miles down the road in Heron Ridge. Probably easily confused. Anyway, not really relevant, as I'm not looking for anyone else. I'm happy with my wife. And I'll miss her like crazy during the week."

"You'll need to get to know some folks, though. Let us know when you're ready to receive visitors, and we'll plan a weekend of debauchery in lesbo heaven."

"How will Sharon feel about that? I thought you two were still in the passionate throes of new-relationship love."

"Call it the seven-month itch. Just kidding. We are still in that whatever you just said."

"Hey, you're the writer. I'm sure you can come up with a better name for it."

Finishing the call with a burst of shared laughter, Peri felt energised enough to tackle the bedroom. Once she'd made up the bed and put her clothes away in the wardrobe, she knew it was all going to work out as planned. Karla was so often away at conferences or on business trips that Peri was used to nights alone. In Heron Ridge, she would have the benefit of beautiful scenery and the delights of nature on her doorstep.

Karla's text arrived just as she was sitting down for a break.

Home and working on a report for Aldo.

She'd try and call her after her meetings on Monday. Peri knew that might not happen. Once Karla got caught up in her work, days went by before she communicated.

Karla's job with ADIT gave them the lifestyle they enjoyed. The mortgage on the house in London was paid off, and the cottage was paid for too. No mortgages to worry about, only the council taxes covered from their joint bank account.

Karla enjoyed her work, and Peri did worry whether or not living in the country would suit her wife. They hadn't really discussed the change in depth. Karla just said she was happy for Peri to follow her dream. Perhaps, like Peri, she would be able to continue working online. Or maybe Aldo would agree to setting up a satellite office in Manchester or Leeds. That could be a solution.

The rain had stopped again, and it looked like it was going to turn into a fine evening. Deciding to give her lungs an airing, Peri stepped outside to survey the garden more closely. The previous owners had put in some flowering shrubs by the wall, separating her property from the farmer's field. She would leave them in, as long as they didn't grow too much and obstruct her view.

There was plenty of room around the side of the house for a vegetable patch. The sun would reach there during the day. The best site for the chicken run was something she might need advice on. Once she was settled in, she would walk up the hill and introduce herself to the farmer. Hopefully, he would be a friendly native. Peri had heard stories about locals not being too accepting of townies whose arrival pushed prices up out of reach of local, first-time buyers. Once they knew she was staying, not just a weekender, that would surely go some way to upgrading her newcomer status.

In bed by nine thirty, hours earlier than her normal time, Peri read for a while before turning out the light. As she snuggled under the duvet, she thought how her routines would change. Early to bed, early to rise. Perhaps she would be woken by the sound of a rooster crowing. She thought of Karla, probably stretched out on the sofa with a glass of Chablis within reach. Peri hoped she'd remembered to eat. She had left a serving of casserole in the fridge to defrost that morning. Instructions for heating were on the counter by the oven. Would Karla even know how to turn it on? She might decide it was too much effort and just order a takeaway.

Peri smiled to herself in the fading light of the strange bedroom and closed her eyes. Sleep overtook her before she had time to make any plans for the morning.

†

Karla hummed to herself as she removed the small case from the back of the bedroom cupboard. With all the packing up of the last few days, Peri hadn't noticed Karla's preparations.

Placing the case on the bed, she unzipped it and threw back the lid. Only a few more personal items to add. For the fifth time, she checked the contents of her small backpack. Passport, euros, phone charger. "No need to bring any toiletries," Syd said. The villa had everything they would need. Sun and sea for ten days. And sex.

Too keyed up to sleep, Karla went into the kitchen and poured herself another glass of wine. She'd binned the casserole in favour of a sushi takeaway. She plopped back on the sofa and started trawling through her Facebook timeline. The thought of Peri mouldering away in the wind and rainswept cottage in Yorkshire flitted by and disappeared. Peri had her dream, time to start living her own.

CHAPTER TWO

Peri slept soundly through the night, exhausted from the exertions of setting up her new home. The unfamiliar sounds of sheep bleating greeted her ears, and she opened her eyes. Reaching for her phone, she saw the time was an unearthly 5:40.

Her normal morning routine was to lie in bed, warm and sleepy, while Karla showered and dressed, always out the door by seven. If she left any later, her commute into the city centre would take half an hour longer.

Peri then followed her own morning rituals, bathroom first, then coffee machine on. A first cup of coffee sustained her while she booted up the laptop and checked her emails, before settling down to write out her list of tasks for the day.

The second coffee of the morning was taken at Costa Coffee, a short stroll away from their house. Ensconced in a comfy corner seat with a double-shot latte and cinnamon toast, she could spend a happy hour with a book. As most of her work time involved editing manuscripts, reading for pleasure was a luxury.

Today was the first day of her new life, and a new routine beckoned. She'd left the coffee machine in the London house, so she would have to make her coffee the old-fashioned way. Peri would use a filter cone and set the kettle to boil. She wondered if Karla would remember to clean out the old coffee grounds before switching on their state-of-the-art Krups coffee maker. *It's my baby, really. I should have brought it with me.* Karla probably wouldn't even bother with it. She'd get her caffeine fix at the office.

A good mental shake brought Peri back to the present and the things that needed doing. She'd sorted out the kitchen already and could devote herself to unpacking her books. That was a task she was looking forward to.

Lying in bed wasn't going to get anything done, and without Karla's lingering scent and warmth to snuggle into, there wasn't any pleasure to be had wrapping herself in the duvet for another half hour's doze.

The sun's rays were already stretching across the expanse of greenery she could see from the kitchen windows, dotted with white, fleecy sheep shapes, some grazing and some still sleeping. A sight to be expected, given the name of the cottage was Sheepfold Grange. From her search of the area on Google Maps, she knew the farm over the hill was called Rushford, probably an established local family with generations of farmers behind them. She wondered if they kept chickens. A regular supply of fresh eggs would be a delight. Maybe they could advise her when she was ready to set up her own chicken run.

Peri opened the kitchen window and took a deep breath, relishing the freshness of the air. She took her coffee and toast into the living room and took stock of the book situation. The built-in bookshelf on one side of the fireplace would be for all her fiction books. The small bookcase she'd brought with her fit nicely in her workspace and could hold the dictionaries, style manuals, and reference books used for her editing jobs.

Karla had moaned about the number of books Peri packed up. Seven boxes in all.

"You're not going to reread all these. Why not leave them here for now?"

"I like to dip into them now and again. And I'll have plenty of time at the cottage for rereading some of my favourites."

She enjoyed arranging the books on the shelves, organising them by author and size. The habit had always amused Karla.

Peri was sweating by the time she unpacked the last box. The sun was fully up over the horizon, and the day promised to be a hot one. She flattened the cardboard container. The collection by the door would have to wait for Karla to return with the car. They'd take the boxes to the tip, along with her other rubbish. Another job. *I wonder if the bin men make it up the lane. I haven't seen the requisite wheelie bin anywhere on the premises. The previous owners wouldn't have taken it with them.* She'd have to call the council.

Registering with a doctor and dentist was also on the task list. She didn't want to have to make the trip back to London for her checkups.

By lunchtime, she had made all the necessary calls. She still needed to see if there was any mail in the box on her way into town. It was at the start of the track to the cottage. She had noticed it when they arrived the day before, but forgot about it with all the unpacking.

Preparing for the journey into the town, Peri checked her bike over and made sure the battery was fully charged. Karla had been dismissive of her choice of transport. "You haven't ridden a bike in twenty years!"

"Once learned, never forgotten. And it's only on country lanes and a canal towpath. I wouldn't dream of riding a bike in the city."

With her lack of experience in mind, Peri attached the battery and took a practice ride around the property. She was relieved to find that it did come back to her and she didn't fall off. She decided she would only need to use the electric power on coming back up the hill, when she'd filled the panniers with shopping.

†

This was scenery to appreciate. Karla stretched out her arms to encompass the expanse of turquoise blue sea reaching to the horizon above a mass of waving palm trees. "I love this."

A hot hand landed on her bare bottom. "So do I."

"I meant the view."

"I like this one." The other hand reached around and positioned itself on Karla's freshly shaved mound. "Are you coming with me?"

Karla shifted her stance to allow the hand access to her pussy lips, which were responding rapidly to the expert touch. "Yesss…" The word dragged out into an extended moan, as first one finger then another entered her warm, wet centre.

Well into their sixth month of clandestine meetings, the intensity of their desire for each other hadn't lessened. Syd could take her to the heights of a screaming orgasm within minutes. Her senses already heightened from arriving on a private jet and being whisked by limo to the villa, high in the hills above the bay, Karla was more than ready for another intense round of lovemaking. Exploring the delights of Monaco could wait. Ten days in paradise.

As she fell back onto the balcony lounger with Syd's breasts inches from her waiting mouth, a fleeting image of Peri in her isolated stone cottage disappeared as quickly as it had arrived. She licked one of the erect nipples in front of her, as the first wave of molten liquid soaked Syd's probing fingers.

Ever since meeting Syd at the company Christmas party, the intensity of the affair they'd started hadn't diminished. At first, Karla couldn't believe the thirty-year-old socialite was going to want anything more than the occasional one-night stand. An eighteen-year age difference was more than enough to fuel an unusual feeling of insecurity, plus the fact that Sydney Louisa Devereaux moved in circles of royalty and A-list celebrities. Karla didn't think a computer nerd like herself could last long in such a rarefied atmosphere.

Syd surprised her at every turn, courting her assiduously.

Peri's dream of living in the country had never been hers, and Karla knew it was time to make the break. The settled domesticity of the past twenty years had lulled her into thinking there was no need to change. She could continue with her secret affairs and still have the comfort of Peri's presence at home.

A night of passion in an anonymous hotel suite had left Karla wanting more. She was approaching fifty. Syd brought her to life with every smouldering look and touch, and Karla wanted to make the most of it while she could. Once she moved into her crone years, no one would look at her twice. She already had to visit her hairdresser twice a month to keep the white hairs at bay.

CHAPTER THREE

Pushing the bike up the hill was hard work. Peri couldn't think what was wrong. The battery had charged up overnight. If she'd known it was going to fail before she reached the top of the hill, she wouldn't have filled the panniers with four bottles of wine and a four-pack of Coronas. The call from Karla had prompted her to stock up. Apologising for missing her the day before, her wife sounded more rushed than usual. She'd been at the airport on her way to a hastily arranged meeting with a potential client in Frankfurt. Karla said she would be back on Friday morning and could make it up to the cottage.

Peri had a menu planned for the lovely summer's evening that it promised to be. Her panniers were also bulging with the necessary food items. Alerted by the sound of a vehicle coming up the lane behind her, she hauled the heavy bike over to the side and cursed as she stepped in a patch of nettles.

The large grey pickup truck stopped, and the driver leaned out of his window. "That looks tough going. Can we give you a lift?"

"Um. Yes, thanks. The battery's gone."

"I'm guessing you're our new neighbour at Sheepfold. I'm Martin."

"Peri."

He opened the door and stepped out. "Here. I'll pop this in the back." He easily lifted the bike and laid it carefully on the bed of the truck.

Peri walked gingerly around to the passenger side, where a small face peered out at her. The mop of curly brown hair over a not-too-clean face made it hard to tell if this was a girl or a boy.

"Move over Bean, give the lady some room," Martin called out.

The child slid closer to the gearshift, while Peri climbed up awkwardly onto the seat.

"Thank you. I was struggling a bit there. I thought the battery was full when I set off today."

"I'm not familiar with these electric things, but maybe you've got a loose connection."

When they reached the cottage, Martin placed the bike against the wall by the front door. The child, Bean, hadn't said a word on the short trip. Dad was more expansive.

"Settling in okay? If there's anything you need, we're just over the ridge."

"Thanks. Are those your sheep I hear in the mornings?"

"Yes. We'll move them further up the hillside soon, so the noise won't bother you for long."

"Oh, I don't mind. It's reassuring to hear some pleasant sounds."

"They're much louder after lambing. Mothers calling to their offspring."

"Oh, have I missed it?"

"Yes. By a few months. Say, why don't you come for supper tonight? Meet the family."

"I couldn't impose…"

"My wife always makes enough food to feed an army. Come on up, any time after five."

"Lovely. Thank you again."

She watched the truck drive away and disappear over the hill seconds later. Turning her attention to the bike, Peri unpacked the panniers and stored everything in the kitchen.

She unhooked the bike battery and took it inside. The leads all seemed secure, but when she switched on the power, the red light flashed ominously. Just what she didn't need. Her only mode of transport, and it looked like she had a dodgy battery. There was sure to be a bike shop in town though. She could manage a manual ride mostly downhill and along the canal towpath.

After a shower and a restorative glass of wine, she Googled cycling outlets and found what she needed. A quick phone call and the helpful sales assistant confirmed that they had what she needed. If she brought in her defunct battery, they would check it out for her as well.

The afternoon was productive. Peri finished up an editing job for one of her favourite authors. It was gratifying when she didn't have to keep referring to the *Chicago Manual of Style* and pointing out to the author all the instances of passive voice in the manuscript.

Although working from home was lonely at times, Peri didn't miss the office environment of her earlier jobs. The constant questions each time a new colleague joined the team soon made her feel like a specimen under a microscope. Had they never met a real-life lesbian before?

Women were the worst offenders. Did she fancy them? If not, why not? Lesbians clearly were expected to jump on any woman they met. Peri was happy to debunk the myth, but it was wearing after a while. As was the curiosity about her love life. What did she do at weekends? Where did she go to meet other muff munchers? That expression came from the men, usually in a sneering tone.

No, working from home had its advantages. The only thing she missed was the proximity of a good café, where she could indulge in a coffee or two and listen in on other people's conversations. She was sure there would be a haven somewhere in the town. It would just take longer to get there either walking or on the bike.

Setting off up the hill at quarter to five with a bottle of Malbec tucked under her arm, Peri wondered how many family members there were if Martin's wife always cooked up a storm. She hoped they weren't having lamb chops, as she stopped at the crest of the hill to watch the sheep grazing in the field.

A black and white border collie rushed towards her when she walked through the gate.

"Radar!" The young voice belonged to Bean. As the child ran forward to control the dog, Peri realised Bean was a girl. Radar stopped in front of her, just as Bean reached them.

"It's okay. He doesn't bite."

Peri nodded and held her free hand out for Radar to sniff. He gave it a friendly lick, wagging his tail all the while.

"See. He likes you."

"That's good."

Bean and Radar fell into step either side of Peri.

"What are we having for tea?"

"Spaghetti bolognese. Rory's choice. Tomorrow night, I choose."

"What will that be?"

"Fried chicken with Chinese noodles."

Peri thought Bean's choice was more adventurous than her brother's. At least the red wine was a good match for a pasta night. The farmyard looked well cared for, and the two-storey stone building was a solid, reassuring sight. The aroma of a rich tomato sauce overlaid the country odours emanating from the barn. Peri guessed that the open window belonged to the kitchen.

The woman who met them at the door didn't fit Peri's stereotyped image of a farmer's wife. Her hair, if not held back in a ponytail, would likely stretch halfway down her back, a deep chestnut colour. Hazel eyes and a wide beaming smile greeted her.

"Welcome to the nuthouse. I'm Hayley."

"Peri. Thank you for having me. Hope this is okay?" She held out the bottle.

"You didn't have to, but thanks. Come on in. Bean, go and wash your hands and root Rory out of his room."

Peri followed Hayley into the kitchen and couldn't help a gasp of surprise. The room was as large as the whole of her cottage, dominated by a wooden table, easily twelve feet long. There were only six place settings at the far end, nearest a picture window. A vista of fields rose up towards the horizon. More sheep grazing.

A Welsh dresser took up part of one wall, holding an array of plates and other tableware. What really caught Peri's eye was the modern look of the appliances. She'd expected an Aga and a wood-burning stove.

"I couldn't be doing with an Aga." Hayley must have read her mind. "We had proper central heating put in when we got married. I told Martin I wasn't living in a draughty farmhouse on top of a hill for anybody. You might want to do the same for Sheepfold. It's fine in the summer, but the winter wind cuts through stone walls like you wouldn't believe possible."

By the time the family had gathered and been introduced, Peri already felt at home with them. Adam, the oldest boy, didn't say much. He obviously worked on the farm and shovelled his food in as if he hadn't eaten for a week.

Rory, the middle child, also said little until Peri told them what she did for a living. Even then, it was Bean who spoke up. "Rory wants to be a writer!"

"What do you write?" Peri asked.

"Some fan fiction."

"That's great. A lot of published authors started that way. It gives you a head start when you do publish your first book, as you'll have an established fan base."

He looked across the table at her then, his eyes alight. "Wow. I hadn't thought of that."

"What are your stories based on?" Peri guessed it wouldn't be Xena.

"*Arrow*. It's an American TV series. A bit like *Batman*, only way cooler, with bows and arrows and awesome technology."

"Sounds like fun."

"Waste of time, if you ask me." Adam gave his brother a withering look.

"I'm not asking you."

There was real venom behind Rory's words, and Peri guessed it was a long-running source of irritation, on both sides.

"All right, boys." Martin spoke quietly. "Save it for later."

"Have you ever wanted to write a novel yourself?" Hayley asked, as she removed their empty dinner plates.

"I haven't really tried. Maybe once I'm settled here, I'll think about it. People say they're going to start writing once they're retired and hardly ever do. It takes a great deal of discipline to sit down every day in front of a blank screen."

The subject Peri hoped to dodge as long as possible didn't arise until they were finishing up the remnants of apple pie and ice cream.

"If you're ever feeling in need of company, please do stop by up here anytime. Adam and I are usually somewhere on the farm or in the fields. I'm sure Hayley wouldn't mind." Martin looked at his wife, and she nodded her agreement.

"That's very kind of you. My partner will be joining me at weekends though."

"Oh. What does he do?"

"Karla is a senior executive in a London-based company. We'll have to do the long-distance thing for a while, until she can complete some of her ongoing projects. We've been together for twenty years, so I expect we'll cope."

"Twenty years." Hayley smiled at her warmly. "Just like us."

Peri relaxed, now that her relationship status was out in the open and the family seemed to accept it easily. She offered to help with the dishes, but Hayley dismissed that suggestion. It was Rory and Bean's turn to do them. Adam disappeared, while the three adults moved into the living room with their wine glasses topped up. Later, Peri couldn't recall what they talked about, but it had been a pleasant way to round off the evening.

Peri was prepared to light her walk back to the cottage with her phone's flashlight, but Martin insisted on letting Adam drive her down. Their exchange of words on the short journey consisted only of a "thank you" on her part and a mumbled "good night" on his. She watched his tail lights disappear over the hill, before going inside.

Tired from the day's activities and the intake of food and wine, Peri only glanced at her phone before collapsing into her bed. Karla hadn't left a message. Peri conjured an image of her wife tapping away on her laptop in a hotel room in Frankfurt, then dropped off to sleep.

†

Rory sat on his bed, hunched over his laptop. The words wouldn't come. Too many other thoughts swirled around. Their new neighbour could be a useful ally in more ways than one, someone he could talk to. Peri seemed approachable, sort of like his Nan. She didn't visit often enough though. Last they'd heard from her, she was at some festival in Cornwall.

Adam was such a dick. Rory had thought starting high school after his older brother left would make life easier. Adam's reputation as a troublemaker followed Rory, and it took two terms for teachers to stop seeing him as a Rushford clone. At least Bean would get a fairer start in September. The only time Rory had a detention was when he forgot his PE kit. That was during the first few weeks of Year 7, so hardly counted as serious misconduct.

If he could just concentrate on this story and forget about the next day's agony that awaited; sitting through double maths and trying not to perv over the new teacher would be torture. Rory was sure his lack of control had been visible to everyone in the class during their last lesson.

He looked at the wall across from his bed. A poster of one of his favourite actors showed off a magnificent bare torso. The poster of a blonde woman astride a dragon barely registered, and only served to fend off any questions from family and friends about his choice of wall art.

Rory closed down his laptop and switched out the light. His hand reached under the covers, as he let his mind drift back to the memory of Mr Stevens bending over to retrieve a pencil from the classroom floor.

CHAPTER FOUR

It was Thursday, but it didn't feel like a Thursday. Dana had missed the midweek break from her routine, when she would meet Peri for lunch in their favourite bistro on Marylebone High Street. Wednesdays had been a creative outlet for both of them. Peri made her laugh with examples of authors' manuscript gaffes. No names, of course. Word substitutions that came under the heading of malapropisms were Dana's favourite. She often used Peri as a sounding board for her own plot problems, or regaled her with the tortuous paths her characters endured on the way to their happy ever after in her latest romance.

She sipped at her second coffee of the morning and gazed at the words on the screen. Ten o'clock, and she'd only achieved a quarter of her word count for the day. No use staring at it if her muse had buggered off. Dana sighed and closed the document. A little Facebook time wouldn't hurt. She'd limit herself to half an hour, or until she finished her coffee, whichever came first. Taking the mug into the living room, she settled on the sofa with her iPad.

Dana heard the front door open and placed her iPad gently on the coffee table, although her first reaction earlier that day had been to throw it against the wall.

"Why are you sitting in the dark?" Sharon flicked the lights on and dropped her briefcase by the door. "What's wrong, honey?" With two quick strides, she reached the sofa and settled next to Dana, pulling her into a life-affirming hug.

"You were so right about Karla," Dana mumbled into her shoulder.

"Oh? What's she done?"

"Just dumped Peri for some bimbo. And Peri doesn't have a clue. I spoke to her yesterday. She's expecting Karla to turn up at the cottage tomorrow evening, to spend the weekend."

"And that's not going to happen…why?"

"Because Karla is sunning herself in exotic climes with said bimbo." Dana sat forward and reached for her iPad. "All over Facebook. See."

Sharon glanced at the screen. Unmistakably, the photo showed Karla Sykes with her arm wrapped around a twenty-something blonde. Both wore bikinis that left nothing at all to the imagination.

"I have to tell Peri, in person. If I set off early in the morning, I can be there by lunchtime."

"Do you even know where this cottage is?"

"Yes, she gave me the address. It has a postcode so the satnav should be able to find it."

"I'd come with you, but I've got client meetings all day tomorrow."

"I know, Shar. Thanks."

Sharon picked up the iPad again. "She looks familiar. And I wouldn't bet on it, but that background looks like south of France, doesn't it? Nice, Monaco..."

"Yeah, could be."

"I bet Ruthie will know who she is. She reads all those *Hello!* type mags. I'll be over at Levi's tomorrow evening, so I'll ask her to have a look."

"Thanks. I wonder how long it's been going on." Dana rested her head in her hands. "And how can I break it to Peri? It'll break her heart."

"Sad to say, but I doubt this is the first time Karla's done this."

"Twenty years they've been together, and married too. I didn't see this coming."

"Well, there is the age difference. How old is Karla? Forty-seven?"

"Forty-eight this year."

"And Peri's sixty. Twelve years might not seem like much when you're in your twenties and thirties. But Peri's getting into pensioner age now."

"Oh, come on. She's still fit and healthy."

"But Karla's coming up to the dreaded five-oh. She might be thinking she needs to make the break now, if she's going to have any chance of trading up for someone younger."

"Shit. That's a blokey attitude if I ever heard one, Miss Greenbaum. Anyway, there's got to be more than a twelve-year age gap with that woman in the photo. She can't be more than thirty."

"If Karla does go down this road she'll no doubt suffer the same heartbreak in a few years. Her looks won't last forever."

"Some women do manage to defy the ageing process. Look at Joanna Lumley or Gillian Anderson."

"Yes, please. Any time." Sharon pulled her into another hug. "But I'd rather have the real thing."

Dana broke contact after a few minutes. "I'm sorry. I've been so wound up about this, I haven't done anything about dinner."

"Good thing I'm not a bloke, expecting my food on the table when I come home from a long day at the coalface. I was thinking we should try that new Indian restaurant on the high street. Set you up for your journey north tomorrow."

"I knew there was a reason I love you."

"My charm and good looks…"

"That too." Dana kissed her on the nose. "Let's go. I'm starving."

"The clichéd starving artist. Did you forget to eat lunch?"

"Well, I didn't feel like it after seeing this. Paced around for a while, then sat down and rammed out four thousand words."

"There you go. Just need a little drama in your life to get your creative juices flowing."

Dana's tummy rumbled loudly. "There are some juices in there that want seeing to. And I don't want this kind of drama every day. At least I won't feel guilty about taking tomorrow off."

"Right. I'll just get out of this power suit and freshen up. We'll be out of here in five."

It was more like fifteen minutes, but as soon as they were walking down the street, arm in arm, Dana relaxed for the first time since she'd seen the photo of Karla and the mystery woman that morning. She could enjoy the evening and the night with her lover. There would be plenty of time on the morning drive to Yorkshire to worry about giving Peri the bad news.

†

Syd's tongue slid over the droplets hovering on the edge of her champagne flute, her eyes raking over Karla's exposed limbs. There was no mistaking her intent, although they'd only left the yacht's stateroom an hour ago.

"Take your top off."

"But...the staff..." Karla waved her arm in the direction of the cabin.

"Nothing they haven't seen before." Syd reached across and ripped the skimpy material away from her breasts. "That's better." Leaning over, she dribbled champagne across Karla's exposed chest.

Any reservations Karla had about being observed melted away at the first touch of Syd's tongue on her nipple. Within seconds, Syd was draped across her body. The pressure on her clit became unbearable, as a hand snaked under the skimpy thong and stroked her into an agonisingly intense orgasm. Her cries could probably be heard across the sea in North Africa.

"Fuck. That feels so good."

Syd brought her fingers up to her face and licked them before putting them against Karla's lips. She opened her mouth to receive the taste of herself, her whole body squirming with desire for more.

"You are such a sexy slut."

Karla moaned as Syd stood.

"Roll over."

Obeying without question, Karla positioned herself face down on the lounger. She couldn't see Syd, but she could hear her fumbling about in the bag she'd brought up on deck earlier.

"Raise your hips." The commanding tone brought another wave of moisture from her vagina. A cushion slipped underneath raised her buttocks in the air. She knew what was coming and cried out again in anticipation.

"Wait for it, baby." Syd used the fingers of one hand to separate her butt cheeks, before positioning the dildo in the other opening. Each thrust with the dildo sent the fingers further up and the combination had her screaming out Syd's name in unison.

Finally at rest, with Syd's length draped across her, Karla's body slowly calmed. Her lover climbed off and unstrapped the dildo, wiping it off and packing it away carefully. She cleaned her hands with the water in the glass.

Karla moved onto her side, her eyes still glazed over from the intensity of her last orgasm.

"Time for lunch, I think. I don't know about you, but I've worked up quite an appetite."

"I'll need another top." Karla raised herself up to a sitting position.

"Oh, I don't think so. I want to see what's on the dessert menu."

"You're insatiable."

"Can't help myself with your body constantly inviting me in." Syd tossed a towel to her. "Wrap up before your tits start to burn. We'll continue where we left off, after some sustenance."

As usual, Karla felt powerless to resist. One thing was certain, she needed to renew her lapsed gym membership if she wanted to keep up with this younger woman. Marathon training was going to be necessary. She followed Syd down into the yacht's spacious dining room, avoiding eye contact with the waiting staff. She only hoped the fish entrées displayed on the table would mask the musk emanating from every pore of her body.

CHAPTER FIVE

No news from Karla. Maybe her plane had been delayed and she couldn't call. Peri tucked her phone back in her pocket and stared out the window. It was a bright sunny day, and she'd planned to make a start on the garden. Motivation was seeping out of her with every passing minute.

She'd tried phoning Karla's office, but all she got was a recorded message. Pulling her phone out again, she scrolled through her contacts list. She did have a number for Karla's sister, somewhere near the end of the alphabet. Yes, Valeria Turnbull. If anything had happened, Valeria might know. Bit of a long shot, as they didn't really see much of each other and Peri had only met her once.

"Hello." The voice on the other end sounded tentative as if expecting a sales call.

"Hi. This is Peri."

"Peri?"

"Karla's partner."

"Oh, yes. Hi. What can I do for you?"

"Just wondered if you'd heard from Karla this week."

"No. She hasn't called here in ages."

"How about her dad? Would she call him?"

"Not too likely. She never visits. All he does when I phone is moan about that and his golf handicap going up."

"Oh, I thought...never mind. I think she's on her way back from a business trip. Sorry to bother you."

Peri ended the call. This was so strange. To her knowledge, Karla made regular visits to Bournemouth to see her ageing father in a nursing home. Each time, she came back saying his condition was deteriorating and he sometimes didn't recognise her.

The knot of worry in Peri's chest was now the size of a football. Where did Karla go if she wasn't visiting an ailing parent?

Before she could give in to the tears that were threatening, a car horn sounded outside. She rushed to throw open the door, relief coursing through her body.

"Darling, I've been so...Dana?"

Her friend was standing with her hand raised to knock, a wary look on her face.

"Surprise!"

"What?"

"I know. I should have phoned ahead. I would have got here sooner, but the satnav took me to three different places. Can I come in? I've brought wine and food."

"Shit, yes. Is Sharon with you?"

"No. Not this time."

Peri led the way into the living room and was immediately pulled into a hug. Dana held on for several minutes before letting go.

"I just need to use the loo, then we'll get stuck in. I'm starving. Why don't you open the wine?"

"It's only eleven thirty."

"So. It's five o'clock somewhere in the world."

Shaking her head, Peri went into the kitchen to collect glasses, plates and cutlery. She opened the wine and poured, leaving a third glass empty for when Karla arrived. Opening the Marks and Spencer's carrier bag, she laid out the contents. Dana knew what she liked and had brought duck-filled wraps for her and egg and cress sandwiches for herself. A large bag of pepper-flavoured Kettle crisps completed the menu.

Dana took a large sip from one of the glasses when she joined her at the small table on the patio. She pointed to the empty glass. "You're expecting Karla?"

"Yes. Any time really. Although, like you, she hasn't phoned."

"Hmm." Dana looked out over the garden and the fields beyond. "This is an amazing spot. I can see why you fell for it."

Peri hadn't thought she was hungry. One bite of a wrap and before she knew it the rest of the first roll had disappeared. They ate in companionable silence, as they often did.

Peri refilled their glasses and sat back, feeling replete. She gave her friend a quizzical glance. "Okay. I'm intrigued as to why you've driven all this way to treat me to lunch. Something that couldn't be discussed by phone or email. Are you and Sharon okay?"

"Oh yes. More than okay. I know you thought I was crazy to move in with her after meeting online and going on three dates, but it just felt so right."

"That's great. So why do I get the feeling something's wrong?"

Dana sighed. She bent down and retrieved her iPad from her bag.

"Don't tell me. You're having trouble with a plot line and want my magic editorial advice?"

"If only." Dana opened her photos app and clicked on an image. "These are screenshots from Karla's timeline. I'm not Facebook friends with her, but Rachel is and saved the pictures for me."

Peri took the tablet and studied the images on the screen. Her brain seized.

Karla was wearing a minimal bikini she'd never seen before, arm around a stunning looking blonde who had the sleek look of a supermodel, also clad in very little material. Both were sporting identical smiles, and Peri recognised Karla's post-sex satisfied expression.

"There are others, if you swipe across to the right."

"I can't..." Peri dropped the tablet on the table and rushed over to the nearest flowerbed. The contents of her stomach covered the nascent marigolds with a projectile of vomit. She stayed bent over, shoulders heaving.

"I'm so sorry. I couldn't not tell you. It's been eating me up ever since Rachel sent me the first screenshot yesterday."

Peri sat back on heels. "Water," she croaked.

"Oh, yeah. Be right back."

It was a perfect day, the kind Peri had imagined enjoying, sitting outside revelling in the beauty of the countryside, savouring the clear, country air. Now, all she could taste and smell were the sour remnants of her lunch. She gulped back the large glass of water Dana handed her and spat out the last mouthful.

Dana took the empty glass out of her hand and gave her a smaller one. "Knock this back. Take the taste away."

Peri sniffed. "I can't drink neat whisky at this time of day."

"Yes, you can. Trust me. I'm a writer."

Closing her eyes, Peri did as she was told. The amber liquid burned its way down her throat. She held out her hand and Dana pulled her up. Steadying herself against her friend's solid frame, Peri took a deep breath.

"Who is that woman? And how long do you think...?" The words stuttered and died.

"Sharon's going round to her brother's this evening. She thinks his wife might have an idea. Ruth reads all those celeb type mags."

"Fucking hell!" Peri paced the length of the garden and back. "Has she been playing me all this time? I talked to her sister just before you came. Seems she hasn't been visiting her poor, old, demented dad at all. He's alive and kicking, playing golf in Bournemouth. What other lies has she told me? Conferences, business trips..."

Her phone pinged and she pulled it out of her pocket. "Oh, god. It's her."

"Let it go to voicemail. She knows you don't answer when you're working."

Peri retrieved the message when the call ended. Karla's voice came through loud and clear. "Hi sweetie. So sorry, there's been a change of plan. I won't be able to make it today. Aldo wants me in Albuquerque to close out a contract. I have to leave in the morning. I'll call you later. Love you."

"Albuquerque. That's a new one."

"Could be credible. I've heard it's becoming the new Silicon Valley. But I'm guessing she's still in Monaco."

Peri picked up the plates from the table and walked into the house. Dana followed with the wine glasses and bottle, placing them on the counter. Peri turned to face her.

"She couldn't just tell me it's over. She's dumped me here. You know, she paid for the cottage. It's in my name, but she paid for it. Tax write off, like her car. That's how she explained it. She was so enthusiastic when we came up to view the property. I thought she really was sharing my dream of living out here. How could I be so stupid?"

"You're not stupid. She's a manipulative bitch."

"I know Sharon never liked her."

"Yeah, well, Sharon's seen it all in her job."

"What do I do now?"

"Do you want to live here?"

Peri walked over to the window and looked out. "Yes, I do."

"Okay. Then we need to put Plan A into action."

"Plan A?" Peri turned back to look at her.

"Give Karla a taste of her own medicine, a little shock and awe. You need to get in first. With Karla away, you can take the initiative. Go back to your house and remove anything you want. Take the car as well. It's in your name, so it's not theft."

"Shit. I haven't driven in twenty years."

"You'll need a car in the winter. It's the perfect vehicle for this area."

"I might be okay driving around here, but there's no way I can bring that thing up the motorway."

"I'll drive it and take a train back."

Peri heaved a big sigh. "I'm so having the coffee machine. And the toaster oven."

"I would start back this afternoon, but I've had too much to drink. Do you have a guest bedroom?"

"Yes, but there are only bunk beds in there. I was planning to replace those with a double or twin beds at some point."

"Okay. Well, bunking down in a bunk bed won't kill me for one night."

Peri sighed again. "I don't want to be alone tonight. Do you think you could cope with being in the same bed with me?"

Dana pulled her into a hug. "No worries. I've brought my lesbian-repelling pjs."

Hopefully, Dana wasn't bored to death with details of what and where Peri wanted to plant, as they wandered around the garden. Her friend let her ramble on, no doubt thinking it would help to take her mind off thoughts of what Karla was doing right then.

Peri fetched her shovel to scrape up the remnants of her lunch along with the deflated marigolds. She threw the load over the wall furthest from the house. No sheep were grazing there, and Peri was sure the next downpour would disintegrate the mess. The damaged marigolds were easily replaced. Not so her broken heart.

Dana did her best to distract her. They played a few games of Scrabble during the evening, but she was easily beaten. Normally, Dana would be crowing over her rare victories, but she only smiled and asked if Peri wanted to play again.

They turned in early and set an alarm for six o'clock. Dana thought they could make it to Peri's house by eleven, at the latest, and had texted Sharon to meet them there.

†

Karla wasn't a big fan of casinos. Aldo had tried to get her to the tables on their one business trip to Las Vegas. This was different. She'd needed little persuading when Syd came out of the bedroom dressed in a tux. She'd provided a strapless black gown for Karla to wear. A slit up the left side revealed her bare legs up to mid-thigh with every movement. Syd hadn't told her where they were going, just ordered her to put the dress on.

"Let's go have some fun." Syd kissed her bare shoulders.

To her surprise, Karla found she was having fun. She sat at the blackjack table, with Syd standing behind her and breathing instructions into her ear. A tap on her right shoulder meant she should take the next card. A tap on the left told her to hold.

Karla didn't know how much time had passed, before Syd gave her the signal to finish. After collecting the winnings from the cashier, they danced and drank more champagne. Karla didn't want the night to end. But, of course, it did.

She stumbled up the steps to the villa. Syd grabbed her from behind and ripped the dress off with one swift motion. Karla shivered at the cool breeze on her bared skin. Syd bent her over the balcony's stone balustrade. Karla moaned into the night air, as Syd's fingers found her wet and wanting. The silhouette of the moon, shining on the sea below, received her cries of ecstasy as she came.

She hoped another night at the casino was on the cards. Soon. Syd led her into the house and continued with a gentler lovemaking in their bed.

CHAPTER SIX

The silence in the house filled Peri with an inescapable sadness. She had only been away a week, but it no longer felt like her home.

Dana and Sharon followed her inside.

"Levi's bringing the van. He'll help move out whatever furniture you're taking." Sharon looked around the living room. "Is there anything you'll want from here?"

Peri opened the Notes app on her phone. "I've made a list." During the sleep-deprived hours of the night she'd gone over the rooms in her head. There were things she had planned to buy for the cottage, thinking it best to leave the furniture in their London house for Karla's use. They'd talked about renting it out for a while, instead of selling up

41

right away. That had been Karla's idea, and Peri realised her wife had never intended to join her at the cottage at all.

"Coffee table, recliner, bookcase, lamps..." Peri sat down on the sofa and looked up at Sharon, her eyes filling with tears. "I'm not sure I can do this."

Sharon perched next to her and took her hands in a comforting hold. "I know it's hard. This is your marital home that you've lovingly cherished. But does Karla? What does it represent for her? A place to come back to when she's finished screwing her latest conquest. Sorry to put it so bluntly."

Peri swallowed back the bile that was rising in her throat. It was true that she had played the happy housewife for all these years. Shopping, cooking, cleaning, laundry...all provided for Karla when she returned from the office, the conference, the business trip. The cosy image of their life together was all built on lies. While Peri had been satisfied with providing a haven for the woman she loved, Karla had been looking elsewhere for something that Peri wasn't giving her. All these years she hadn't really been a wife, more a mother substitute.

"I see this kind of thing all time in the divorce cases I handle. The erring partner isn't going to change their ways."

"Oh my god!" Dana charged into the room. "Look what I found in the desk drawer." She dropped a fistful of phones encased in plastic sandwich bags onto the coffee table in front of Peri. "They're labelled with different names."

"She uses different phones when she travels on business."

"I'm sure that's what she's told you. But what business does she have with Marli, Britta, Hester, and so on?"

Peri picked up one of the bags and inspected the label. Joyce. She turned over another one. Lacey. There were seven in all.

Taking a deep breath, she looked at her friends. "Right, let's do this." She got to her feet. "Kitchen first."

By the time they had piled all the items from Peri's list by the door, Levi arrived with the van. It was a small transit, but they were able to fit in the bulk of the furniture. Peri had added the bed and the bedside tables from the guest room.

Smaller items, including the printer, were loaded in the Range Rover. Peri filled a suitcase. She had left clothes behind, thinking she would need them for occasional visits to the city. Much as she would have liked to enact a vicious attack on Karla's wardrobe or leave a highly visible message on the bathroom mirror, Sharon advised against such behaviour.

"Keep to the moral high ground. You've done nothing wrong. Don't give her anything to use against you."

"I'll take one last walk around the house to see if there is anything I've forgotten." Peri stood in their bedroom for the last time. She suddenly remembered the present she'd bought. Karla's birthday wasn't until September, but Peri had found the perfect gift back in February and stored it in the drawer under the bed. She pulled the drawer open and took out the package from the jewellery store. She had envisioned the expensive necklace settled against Karla's smooth, olive skin, contrasting with her black hair. She'd stared through the store window and enjoyed the fantasy of placing it around her wife's neck, prior to going out to a restaurant for a celebratory dinner. *Total fiction.* When was the last time they had done that for any occasion? She tucked the bag into her pocket and walked out to join her friends by the front door.

They travelled in convoy back to Dana and Sharon's house, with Dana driving the Range Rover, Levi in the van and Sharon in her car. Levi declined the offer of a drink and left to spend the evening with his family.

Sinking back, at last, into the comfortable armchair, Peri relaxed for the first time that day. Dana set a large glass of red wine on the table next to her.

"I'm ready for this." Peri reached for the drink and took a large gulp. "Thank you both so much. I couldn't have done any of it on my own. Hell, I wouldn't even have thought of doing anything like this."

"I still think you should have left some prawns decomposing under the floorboards." Dana sipped her own wine.

"Good thing I'm here to keep you two in check." Sharon sat down next to Dana on the sofa. "Like I said earlier, keep to the moral high ground. With any luck, we'll manage a no-contest divorce."

"I didn't get a chance to thank your brother properly. It was so good of him to give up a Saturday afternoon to help out."

Sharon smiled at her. "The end of the football season always leaves him with free time on Saturdays and Sundays. He's a season ticket holder at Tottenham. He obviously expected his son to join him. When David was born, Levi couldn't wait for him to be old enough to go to matches with him. It nearly broke his heart when the lad finally admitted he wasn't interested. Luckily, Naomi has proved to be an enthusiastic fan of the game."

"How old are the kids?"

"David's eleven, and Naomi will be eight this year."

Peri returned her empty wine glass to the table. "Have you ever thought about having children?"

Dana snorted wine through her nose and Sharon laughed. "No. I've always been happy with having a career, without that kind of distraction. We might have to get a cat though, to help Dana fulfil her maternal instincts."

"Ha ha. Very funny. More wine, anyone?"

Peri accepted a top-up. With the various strains of the day, she hoped a few glasses of wine would help her sleep through the night.

†

Karla could barely keep her eyes open. She may have dreamed of living a hedonistic lifestyle, but it was exhausting. Her nearly fifty-year-old body was struggling to keep up. Syd had no such trouble. She was a Duracell bunny on steroids, never running down. The coke she snorted at regular intervals kept her going. Karla had declined. Sniffing a few lines wasn't her drug of choice, and the gin and tonics she craved would only reinforce her need for sleep.

Going back to work would seem restful after this trip.

CHAPTER SEVEN

Dana checked her rearview mirror again, to make sure Sharon had followed when she turned off the main road. "I can't believe you thought you could manage up here with just an electric bike." Dana glanced over at her friend, slumped against the passenger door. Peri had dozed for a good part of the journey, no doubt making up for lack of sleep the past two nights.

Peri roused herself and looked around. "Well, I thought Karla would be here at the weekends, and we'd do a weekly shop."

Dana stopped herself from saying, *and you thought she would want to do that.* Karla probably hadn't stepped inside a supermarket or grocery store of any description in all the time she'd lived with Peri. With a shake of her head, Dana drove the vehicle into the enclosed yard in front of the cottage and turned off the engine.

"It's lovely to drive. I don't think you'll have a problem getting used to it." She opened the door and stepped down onto the path.

"I still think it's too big for me. I only really need a runaround." Peri walked stiffly around to the back and opened the boot.

Sharon parked the van next to them and got out. Dana enjoyed the sight of her lover's breasts as she stretched her arms above her head, working out a few kinks from the long drive.

"Stop perving, Churchill. We've got work to do." Sharon playfully slapped her butt, as she walked past to help Peri unload the Range Rover.

Peri busied herself with setting up the kitchen, while Dana and Sharon sorted out the furniture. Sharon proved adept at figuring out how the bunk beds were put together. Between them, they soon had them in pieces. Peri joined in to take everything out to the garage. She could ask Hayley if she knew anyone who would like to have them. Otherwise she'd be asking the Rushfords for another favour to make a trip to the tip.

It took the three of them to wrestle the double bed up the stairs. At one point, Peri thought she'd have to ask Martin and Adam to come and help.

"How many lesbians does it take to move a bed?" Dana grunted when they finally made it into the room. Sharon demonstrated her advanced DIY skills by installing the headboard.

"I didn't know you were so butch," Peri joked.

Dana grinned at her partner. "Oh yeah. That and the power suits she wears to work are why I keep her around."

Peri gave them a wan smile and left them to sort out the bedding. She heard Sharon say to Dana, "That was a bit insensitive, my love."

She didn't hear her friend's response, but she knew Dana hadn't meant to upset her. Back in the kitchen she set up the coffee machine and found places for the extra cookware she'd brought. A wine rack was going to be one of her next purchases. The one from the London house was too modern looking, and she wanted something that would be more in keeping with the cottage decor.

Sharon had insisted on making a stop at Waitrose before they left the outskirts of the city, shocked to learn that the supermarket didn't have many outlets in the north. There were none anywhere near Sheepfold Grange. Peri unloaded the groceries, keeping out the items needed to prepare their evening meal.

They'd decided to keep it simple and opted for a selection of curry ready-meals. Sharon and Dana appeared in the doorway, just as she'd finished setting out the onion bhajis, olives and naan.

"Beer or wine?"

"Oh beer, definitely. I'm parched."

"Goes better with curry anyway," Sharon added.

Peri indicated the dishes on the counter. "Take these out to the patio, and I'll bring the drinks. Might as well enjoy the last rays of the sun."

"I can see the attraction." Sharon gazed out over the valley. "But I don't think I could live here. Maybe a holiday now and then."

"You're welcome anytime. Now you've got a proper bed as well."

"We'll take you up on that, I'm sure."

Peri looked away, as Sharon reached for Dana's hand. She knew they were trying not to show overt displays of affection in front of her, but they were so obviously in love that they had a hard time keeping their hands off each other. When had she and Karla lost that spark? Too long ago for her to recall.

"Ready for the main course?"

"Sure. And another round of beers."

Dana followed her into the kitchen to get the drinks. Peri pulled the boxes out of the fridge and started to prepare them for heating in the microwave.

"Here. Let me do that. You take the beers out."

"Are you sure?"

"Yeah. You look done in."

"I know. I look like shit, and I feel like shit. But I'm glad you're here. Thanks for doing all this. I don't know how I can repay you."

Dana pulled her into a hug. "Don't even think about it. That's what friends are for." She put the first box into the microwave and set the timer. "You might want to start saving for Sharon's divorce fee though."

†

Karla swallowed the water, trying not to gulp it down. She didn't want another bout of hiccups. Not a sexy sound.

The combined effects of the heat and the amount of alcohol consumed the previous night made hydrating essential. She'd found a shady spot to sit, where a slight breeze drifted in from the sea. At least the pounding in her head had simmered down to a light headache.

Syd was at the other end of the villa's extensive garden, pacing up and down, talking into her phone. She ended the call and sauntered back to Karla. From the look on her face, it had possibly been bad news.

"I have to go into the town. Damian's asked me to collect something for him. Shouldn't take too long."

Syd's older brother had phoned a few times in the past week. Karla sat up. "I'll come with you."

"No. You stay here. You're looking a bit peaky."

"Just a slight headache. It's clearing up."

"Still, no need for you to come. Just relax." Syd bent down and kissed her forehead. "Save your energy for later."

Syd's smile left no mystery as to what later might entail. Karla's insides jolted at the promise of a return to the bedroom. Or maybe the dining room table. The memory of Syd licking the remnants of their late-night supper off her body, as she lay spreadeagled amongst the glasses and cutlery, surged through her mind, creating more turmoil in her belly.

Her facial expression must have triggered the same memory for Syd.

"Hold that thought. I'll be back soon." She walked away with a deliberate sway of her hips that gave Karla another visual image to arouse more pulsations in her lower abdomen. Her shorts were wet before Syd reached the doorway. More water and a dip in the pool would sort out both her headache and the other ache that seemed to need constant attention.

She wriggled out of her clothes and slipped into the warm water. She hoped Syd wouldn't be away too long.

CHAPTER EIGHT

Dana settled in the chair next to Sharon on the patio, followed by Peri who sat down on the other side. A collective sigh met the morning air, as they all enjoyed the aroma of freshly brewed coffee and the view spread out in front of them.

"I thought we'd be woken by a rooster at dawn. Glad we weren't though." Dana breathed in a lungful of the freshness surrounding them.

"Oh, you'll hear him all right, but he's a late riser. Doesn't start crowing before noon."

"I can see why you want to live here, Peri," Sharon said. "But it would never have suited Karla."

"I thought we weren't going to mention the K word so early in the day." Dana pinched her lover's knee.

"Sorry, I'll be on my way after I finish this. There are a few things we need to talk about before I go."

"What else is there?" Peri sighed.

Dana watched her friend with a critical eye. She'd hugged Peri in the kitchen, while they were waiting for the coffee to brew. Peri had been on the verge of tears, and the bags under her eyes indicated another sleepless night. Although Sharon had to go back to London, Dana was glad she could stay on to give her friend some much needed moral support.

"Well, finances for one. Do you have a joint bank account?"

"Yes. For paying household bills. They all go out on direct debit. I put in five hundred a month as my contribution."

"Okay. You can stop the deposits and change the passwords on any other accounts you have."

"Do I need to go into a bank here and move my account from Putney?"

"No. It doesn't really matter these days where your physical bank is. You do all your banking online, don't you?"

"Yes, and I have a PayPal account for my business payments and expenses."

"Good. Just to be on the safe side, I would suggest you change your password on that too."

Peri gulped back some coffee. "What are you doing with Karla's phones?"

"There's a PI we use, who specialises in things like this. He can extract the data. If she's just used an unencrypted messaging app, it will be fairly simple to retrieve any communications she's had with these women."

"Really?"

"Yes. Most PI work nowadays is done on computer. They don't have to slink around in backyards, surreptitiously taking photos. People do it for them, as we've seen. They post their lives online, videos on YouTube even. The age of the selfie." Sharon took a sip of her own coffee. "There's something else I'll ask him to look at. I would guess she's used some dating sites. She won't have met all these women at conferences. I think it might be a good idea to take a look at her computer as well. Is it password protected?"

"Yes. However, as far as I know, it's still the one she's always used…KhameLion21."

"Can you spell that for me?" Sharon tapped the characters into her phone. "Caps on K and L?"

"Yes."

"Okay. Good. We'll take a look when we return the phones."

"You're putting them back?"

"We don't want to alert her to how much we know of her activities. Also, we're not taking anything out of the house that is solely her property. That would be stealing. So, is there anything else you want from there?"

"No. I don't think so."

"You've got all the documentation you need for the car and the cottage. They are both in your name, aren't they?"

"Yes."

"What about the house?"

"That's joint."

"Okay, so if she sells it, you will be entitled to half."

"Won't she be able to fight this? I mean, she'll have proof that she actually paid for the car and the cottage."

"Yes, but she's given them to you and put them in your name."

Peri stood and walked away from the patio. She stopped when she reached the low stone wall separating her garden from the field. A few sheep were grazing there.

Dana moved to follow, but Sharon restrained her. "It's a lot to take in. I think she needs some time to process. It's good that you'll be here." She leaned in for a kiss, just as her phone pinged.

"Shit. Better not be work." Sharon glanced at the screen. "Oh, it's Levi. Hah. Ruthie's come through and put a name to that woman Karla's cavorting with on Facebook. One Sydney Louisa Devereaux. Hmm. Karla is moving in exalted circles. Seems Sydney hangs out with some of the younger royals. And the location, as we thought, is Monaco." She pinged off a quick thank you message. "I'll look her up when I get home. May be useful to have some background info on her."

"None of this is going to make Peri feel any better."

"No. I guess not. So, what are you going to do with her today?"

"She's probably not in the right state of mind for a driving lesson, but I thought maybe a drive out somewhere to get an overview of the area. Try and take her out of herself for a bit."

"Good thinking. I'd better get going. I've got a pile of case notes to review before tomorrow."

Dana watched the van disappear down the lane, waving and blowing a last kiss, knowing Sharon could see her in the wing mirror. When she returned to the house, Peri was in the kitchen washing up their breakfast dishes.

"I'm sorry. I should have said goodbye." She spoke without turning around.

"It's okay. She understands."

"You guys have done so much for me. How will I ever repay you?"

"Don't even think about that. What are friends for? We're here for you."

Peri turned then and collapsed into Dana's waiting embrace. "How could she do this? All this time. I just don't understand what I did wrong."

There were no comforting words she could think to offer, so Dana held on until Peri's sobs subsided. When she could pull back, she said, "How about we take a drive out somewhere? Find a nice country pub for lunch?"

Peri swiped at her face with a dishtowel. "Okay. As long as you're driving."

"Of course."

†

A change of scene was working its magic. Peri gazed at the expanse of moorland stretching out to the horizon and felt her mood lightening with each passing mile. "Oxenhope Moor. I read that, on a clear day, you can see across to Blackpool from up here."

"That can't be true. It must be at least fifty miles away."

"Well, that's what it said. From the highest point."

Dana kept her eyes on the road as it wound its way downhill. "So, where to? Haworth is coming up. Or we could carry on to Skipton."

"Might as well try Skipton. I don't think I can face the Brontës right now."

The popular market town was already busy, and all the car parks were full. They drove on to find Settle was also bustling, but they did find a parking space.

"You know, we're almost in Cumbria here."

"I've never been to the Lake District." Peri took in a lungful of fresh air, as she stepped out of the vehicle. "Lots of good walking there, I guess."

"Are you going to join a walking group?"

"It's on my list of things to do."

"It is beautiful here." Dana took in the stone-built houses and shops, the trees lining the streets, and the steep hills reaching up to the sky." I don't think I'm ready to move away from London just yet. What was that saying about if you're tired of London, you're tired of life?"

"Samuel Johnson. 'When a man is tired of London, he is tired of life.' He also said something about you wouldn't find an intellectual willing to leave the city."

"I suppose country living wasn't too idyllic back in those days. They wouldn't have had running water or electricity on their farms."

"True."

They had reached the central part of the town and stood looking around.

"Ah, I think I've heard of that place over there. Ye Olde Naked Man Café. Do you want to go in? We could have a coffee. It's too early for lunch."

After coffee and a shared, freshly baked, blueberry muffin, they headed out to explore the town. Peri was particularly taken with the well-organised bookshop. She bought a book she'd been wanting for some time. A climb up a hill through the park, and they found a place to sit and admire the view.

"I'll have to come back and take the steam train sometime."

"Where does it go?"

"To Carlisle and back. The scenery is supposed to be spectacular."

"Okay. Let's plan it for one of the times Sharon and I come up to visit."

"So, the countryside is growing on you, is it?"

"Yeah. Like I said. I can see the appeal. I just don't think I could live here full time."

"I might be able to convert you."

"You'll get more than a toaster oven if that happens. It's all lovely on a summer's day like this, but will you still be so enthused come wintertime?"

"I'm sure winter has its charms too."

"What? Like the cold wind and rain whistling up your nether regions while you're milking the goats."

"I'm not having goats."

†

The drive back didn't seem to take as long. Dana thought it was probably because she knew where she was going. They stopped to fill up with petrol, and Peri went inside the shop to pay. Dana switched the engine back on and moved the car forward, to let the one behind get access to the pump. She reached over to switch off the navigation, when a thought struck her.

The Destinations option revealed a list of programmed sites. Glancing through the windscreen, Dana could see there were still two other people ahead of Peri in line for the cash register. Dana took photos on her phone, scrolling down the list to capture them all. She rang Sharon.

"Hey, babe. Everything ok?"

"Yeah. We've been for a drive out and stopped for petrol on the way back. I've just realised there's some more info we can get from the satnav. There's a whole list of destinations stored on the in-car system."

"Good thinking, Batman."

"I've taken pics. As soon as we get back to the cottage I'll send them to you."

"Great. It's all good ammo. Maybe you should be writing detective novels instead of soppy romances."

"Don't knock them. It's the romance that sells. How was the drive back?"

"Surprisingly hassle free for a Sunday. How's Peri doing?"

"Better than she was this morning. I don't think I'll tell her about the satnav though. No point adding to her distress."

"Of course. Love you loads. I'll call you later." After making smootchie kissing noises, they both ended the call.

Peri climbed back into the passenger seat, as Dana closed her phone.

"Just checking in with Sharon. She had a good drive."

Neither of them felt like eating anything after the late, and very filling, lunch they'd had at the pub. They sat on the patio. Peri sipped her coffee, lost in thought.

"Are you sure Karla won't have changed her password? Aren't computer geeks obsessed with security? That last school Lindsay worked at, the teachers all had to change their passwords every month. Drove her mad."

"I liked Lindsay. Do you still hear from her?" Peri sipped her drink.

"No. She moved to Devon. Last I heard she was dating a naval officer."

"Hm. I guess you wouldn't be able to compete with a hot woman in a uniform." Peri set her empty mug on the table. "Of all your exes, I did like Lindsay."

"All my exes! Come on, there aren't that many."

"More than I've had. Anyway, in answer to your question about passwords. She does have a notebook she writes them in. For banking and other sites she uses. Top left-hand drawer of the desk, I think."

"Oh great. Do you mind if I call Sharon to let her know?"

"No, of course not."

Sharon answered on the second ring. "I was just going to call you."

"Right, well, we were talking about other passwords Karla might have. It seems she's broken the rule usually drummed into us and has written them down in a notebook. We could probably access her bank account."

"We could. But we don't want to leave a trail. If we're lucky, she may have saved some bank statements. We'll check out the files anyway."

Peri picked up their mugs and went into the kitchen for refills. When she returned, Dana's phone was on the table.

"That was a short call."

"I didn't want to keep her from the bath she's been looking forward to."

"Sorry you're stuck here with me." Peri placed the mugs on the table and sat. "I'm sure you'd rather be there to scrub her back."

"Yeah." Dana sighed.

"Thank you for being here. I know I've said it before, but it is helping."

"You're stronger than me, Peri. I think I would have crumbled into a heap of dust if my partner of twenty years had done this to me. I mean, I've written romances with loads of angst, but there's always a happy outcome. I know it's going to happen."

"She's ruined my memories of what I thought were the best years of my life. Not just ruined, shit all over them."

Dana gave her leg a squeeze. "Hey. Don't let her wreck the rest of your life. The best may be yet to come."

Peri stared into the distance and and let her thoughts roam again. They drank their coffee, watching the few sparse clouds moving slowly across the deep blue sky. Peri stood finally and stretched.

"Come on. Before you fall asleep, I'll show you where I want to put in a pond."

"A pond? I thought you were going to have chickens."

"That was my original plan. But after talking to Hayley, it doesn't seem sensible. She's feeding a family of five and still has more eggs than she can use. What would I do with mine? I don't eat eggs every day. I'm going to concentrate on growing veg. Martin's offered to help erect a greenhouse."

"Wow, really. You're lucky to have such good neighbours. I'm glad you're not totally isolated here. We were worried you would find it too lonely."

"Too much to do in the summer. Winter might be a different proposition." Peri put that thought to the back of her mind and led Dana across the lawn to the spot she thought would be ideal for a pond.

CHAPTER NINE

Dana entered the kitchen to find Peri preparing the coffee machine for their first cups of the day.

"Morning. This won't take long. Did you sleep all right?"

"Yes. I'm glad we brought that bed. Slept like a log." Dana noted the dark circles under Peri's eyes, evidence that she hadn't slept much at all.

A knock at the door startled them both. "Who could that be? You don't get Jehovah's Witnesses coming round here, surely."

"Oh, it might be one of the Rushfords delivering eggs."

Dana opened the door and came face to face with a woman holding an egg box. Taking in the alert green eyes and abundance of chestnut hair, she thought if this was a farmer's wife she just might be tempted to move to the country too.

"Hi. These are for Peri."

"Thanks. I'm Dana."

"Oh. Hayley."

"Don't tell me. You thought I was Karla."

"Yes, well. I saw the car and wondered."

"Just a friend. Do you want to come in? The coffee is fresh."

"Thanks. But I've got a few more deliveries to make."

Dana watched her walk back to her car. The rear view was pretty enticing as well.

"So, I can see the attraction of living here." Dana smirked at Peri and placed the egg box on the counter.

"Fresh eggs, yes, definitely a plus."

"Not that, you twit. The farmer's wife. What a hottie? You kept that quiet."

"Don't even go there. Anyway, I thought you and Sharon were still all loved up."

"We are. That doesn't limit my ability to appreciate a fine-looking woman when I see one."

Peri opened the box. "How do you want yours cooked?"

"Whatever's easiest."

"Okay." Peri took out two eggs and cracked each one single-handedly into the frying pan.

"Wow. Where did you learn to do that? I usually end up with eggshell everywhere and the drippy stuff all over my hands."

"One of my housemates at uni was training to be a chef. Probably the most useful thing I learned during the entire five years."

"Hey, I think obtaining a Masters degree in English Lit means you were paying attention in other lessons too."

Peri sniffed and turned her attention to the eggs in the pan. "Over easy?"

"Yes."

She gave them an expert flip and waited a few moments before lifting them out onto the plates.

Dana mopped up the last splash of yolk with her toast. "So this is what real, farm-fresh eggs taste like."

"Yeah. Straight from the chicken's bum this morning to your plate."

"Not sure I want to think of it quite like that."

Peri took another sip of her coffee. "You know, during the night, I was thinking back over the last few years. Karla and I haven't been out for dinner on our own for a long time. We used to go at least once a week. I'd go and meet her after work. Sometimes we'd see a film or a play. When did it stop? Ten years ago, maybe. Is this all my fault? Did I become too complacent?"

"None of it's your fault." Dana stood. "I'll wash up, and we'll go hit the town. You can show me the delights of this lesbo heaven."

"Not much will be open before ten."

"Okay. Ideal time to start your driving lessons, I think."

"I'm not sure I'm ready for that."

"You can't put it off forever. It's a clear day. There won't be much traffic on the road at this time, and you can take advantage of my expert instruction."

"On the road," Peri squeaked. "I was thinking of just tooling up and down the lane."

"We'll start with that. Before I leave tomorrow, you need to be confident of handling it in traffic."

"I won't be taking it far. And I'm going to trade down to something smaller as soon as I can."

"Good idea. But you'll want something sturdy enough to handle that hill in the winter."

"I was thinking of a Golf or a Jazz. Maybe even an automatic."

"Guess you didn't do much sleeping last night."

"No. You know what it's like when things just keep churning around in your mind. I'm glad I don't have any jobs on at the moment. I don't think I could concentrate on anything for long."

Dana collected their plates. "Good thing I'm here then."

Before they even reached the main road, Peri was a nervous wreck. "I'll never get the hang of the gears. Please, Dana. I think you should take over. I don't want to stall in the middle of traffic."

"You're doing fine."

"Well, it's not like riding a bicycle. I've forgotten everything I ever knew about driving."

"It'll come back, but you will need to practice." Dana checked the road for oncoming cars. "You're good to pull out now. There's nothing coming. You'll be fine on this stretch. It's zoned at twenty miles per hour. You'll not be holding anyone up. Well, you will, but you'll be saving them from a speeding fine if there are any camera vans lurking."

When they finally reached the town and Peri had safely parked in a space on a side road, she let out the breath she'd been holding for the last mile.

"Definitely a good time to come. Looks like parking will be a nightmare later on." Dana patted Peri's knee. "You did good. It'll get easier."

"I hope so. I don't need the stress."

They walked around looking in shop windows and finally decided on a café, of which there were many to choose from.

"I know this place has won awards for having a large proportion of independent businesses, but it seems to be mainly cafés and charity shops." Dana opened the door, and the smell of freshly brewed coffee wafted out. "I've heard there's a lesbian wine bar, though."

"How is it that you know more about what's going on here than I do? You're the visitor."

"Not hard. You just have to Google it."

Dana ordered two cappuccinos, while Peri ventured over to the comfortable seats by the window.

"They have some good-looking cakes. Do you want to share one?"

"Yeah, okay. You choose."

By the time they finished the lemon drizzle cake and Peri had scraped the last of the froth out of her cup, she was feeling more relaxed. "I think I should take some of that cake back. It's delicious."

"Good thinking. Half a piece wasn't really enough."

The café was doing good business. Most of the patrons appeared to be regulars coming in for their caffeine fixes. One looked like she might be a student typing an essay on her laptop. She had books and papers spread across two tables pushed together. Another was concentrating on their screen with an intensity Peri recognised from watching Karla work at home. He could be designing a website or coding an app. She was used to seeing this in London coffee shops, usually wall to wall with people on their various devices. It was unusual to find a wi-fi-free zone anywhere. Everyone wanted to be connected, every hour of the day. She had thought it might be different out here in the countryside, but clearly not.

Dana finished her coffee and clattered the cup down onto the saucer. "Great spot for people watching. I'm sure I've seen at least three gay couples, and a dyke has just gone into that health food store."

"Honestly. How can you tell?"

"You just can. Your gaydar's been out of action for too long. You'll pick it up again if you sit here long enough."

"I won't be spending all my time sitting in cafés."

"Right. Of course. You'll be too busy growing your organic veggies. There's a Co-op over there. Do you need to pick up any groceries while we're here?"

"Food, no. But you two finished off the beer."

Peri drove back after they'd done the shopping. She still didn't feel comfortable driving. It would take more practice, but she was glad she'd made a start. She wasn't sure why she'd thought she could manage without a car. Years of city life had sheltered her from the realities of country living.

CHAPTER TEN

The paper continued to pile out of the printer at an alarming rate. Peri resisted looking at the printed pages until the machine had finished its work. The final three pages took some time. Peri didn't really want to see the full-colour photos of Karla, but couldn't avoid them when they opened on the screen. There she was lounging on a yacht drinking champagne, then reclining by a pool with an expanse of Mediterranean Sea in the background. Another showed her sitting at a blackjack table with the mystery woman, who looked incredibly sexy in a tux. All of the photos were posted on Facebook with the dates and times showing. The more evidence the better, Sharon had said in her accompanying email.

Peri carried the stack of paper into the living room and placed it carefully on the coffee table, face up. Another cup of coffee was needed before she could face the evidence. Preparing a double-shot latte helped calm her nerves. Once she was seated again, she picked up the first page and started to read messages sent to a woman called Britta, setting up meetings. Peri didn't need to consult her calendar to know they corresponded with evenings Karla had claimed to be working.

Flicking through the pile, she found another name, Marli. They'd enjoyed a longer assignation during the so-called conference in Sweden. Karla had brought back a Moomin love mug for Peri, apologising for having bought it at the airport. There hadn't been any time out during the conference to do proper shopping.

Peri put the pages down and finished her coffee. She walked out onto the patio and let her tears fall, blurring the view.

How could she have been so blind? The signs had all been there. But she wasn't looking. Karla always showered when she came home late, saying she needed to wash off the city grime. She'd needed to wash away the evidence of another woman's scent, the musky odour Peri would have recognised immediately.

She did know what some people thought of their relationship. She was punching above her weight. What was a stunner like Karla, with her exotic Spanish looks, doing with an obviously older plain Jane like Peri?

But it had worked, or so she'd thought for all their twenty years of living together. Their personalities blended well. Peri's calm tempered Karla's fiery passions. Perhaps that should have been a clue that Karla would never be truly content with a settled lifestyle. Work hard, play hard, was a motto she subscribed to and was certainly encouraged by Aldo's company ethos.

Peri enjoyed quiet evenings at home, reading or listening to music. When Karla was actually at home, she spent much of the time on her office computer or sitting on the sofa and constantly fiddling with her phone. She'd probably been sending these text messages, now collated by Sharon's colleague for use in the divorce proceedings.

Any thoughts she'd harboured, during the long hours of sleeplessness, of not going through with the divorce, evaporated along with her tears. She couldn't kid herself that Karla would change. This had been going on too long, with too many other women.

Her phone pinged with a text from Dana.

On the London bound train. Running to time.

Peri texted back a smiley face.

She already missed having her friend around. Dana's presence had stopped her brooding too much. There were jobs she could be getting on with, starting with the vegetable patch she'd planned out.

Another sound from her phone indicated an incoming email. She opened a message from the mainstream publisher she worked for, with the next manuscript requiring her services attached. Peri was thankful for the science fiction novel. She couldn't have faced ploughing through a lot of angst, when her own HEA was crumbling into dust around her feet.

Peri restocked the printer with paper and set it off. Printing the novel would use up most of her last ream. She could place an order online or maybe she should buy from the newsagents in town. One more advantage of having a vehicle. Thinking of that reminded her she wanted to speak to the Rushfords about driving lessons.

Peri parked the Range Rover in front of the barn and switched off the engine. It took her a moment to remember to put the handbrake on.

Hayley greeted her at the door of the farmhouse. "That's a lovely car. I thought you didn't drive."

"Well, that's why I'm here. I haven't driven since passing my test forty-two years ago. Dana drove it up for me and got me started before she went home yesterday, but I think I need more practice. I wondered if you or Martin would mind giving me a few lessons."

"I'm sure between us we can. I've just made a pot of coffee. Would you like some?"

"Oh, yes. Thank you. My nerves are shot from just driving up the lane to here."

Once they were settled at the table with coffee and a plate of freshly baked brownies between them, Peri remembered to ask about deliveries.

"Do you get online deliveries up here?"

Hayley shook her head. "No. They tend to get lost and just dump items on someone else's doorstep. Easiest option is to collect from the Post Office."

"Oh good. I was also wondering about rubbish. I haven't seen a wheelie bin anywhere."

"We used to have them at the end of the track by the post boxes, but they kept blowing over. We just make regular trips to the tip. If you want anything taken, just leave it by your gate."

"That's kind. Once I get used to driving again, I'll be able to do that myself." Peri bit into a brownie, still warm from the oven. "Mmm. Delicious."

"Thank you. It's my own recipe." Hayley sipped her coffee. "Martin said it looked like you'd brought more furniture when he drove past yesterday."

"Yes, Dana and her partner helped me move some things from the London house." Peri set her coffee cup down on the table, dismayed to find tears welling up.

"What's wrong?" Hayley reached over and placed a hand on her arm.

"Everything." She swallowed and looked into Hayley's warm, green eyes. "Karla won't be joining me here. Our marriage is a sham, and I didn't see it coming."

"What's happened?"

"Where to start? She lied about where she was last week, telling me she was going on business trips, first to Frankfurt, then to the States. She is actually in Monaco with another woman. I only know this because a friend of a friend saw the photos she posted on Facebook."

"'Oh god. I'm so sorry."

"It's not the first time. Seems she's been doing this for many years. I always accepted she had to be away for her work, weeks at a time if they were carrying out due diligence audits on companies that were being taken over. Some of these were probably real. She wouldn't have lasted long at the company otherwise."

"Did she ever sleep with men?"

"No. She's always been proud of being a gold-star lesbian."

"Gold star?"

"Yes. Only ever slept with women. She's very dismissive of bisexuals. Says they need to make their minds up. I don't go along with that view. You love who you love."

"Are you a gold-star as well?"

"More of a bronze, I'd say. I went out with a few boys in high school, although we never went all the way. I didn't figure it out until I was at uni."

Hayley nodded thoughtfully, sipping her coffee. "I guess my mother didn't figure it out until later in life. Maybe she did know before my dad left. Maybe that's why he left. She never said, just got on with raising me on her own."

"Your mum's a lesbian? Do the kids know?"

"Adam suspects, I think. He's always a bit standoffish with her, but we've not told them. That's for her to do. She's never brought any girlfriends here." Hayley winced. "That's a weird term isn't it? I can't grasp the thought of my mother having girlfriends at her age."

Peri stared into her empty coffee mug. "We must be about the same age. At least she hasn't made the mistake of getting married to one of them." She could feel tears gathering again.

"Have you got a good lawyer?"

"Yes. Sharon, Dana's partner, specialises in divorce." Peri sniffed. She really didn't want to start crying again.

Hayley patted her arm sympathetically. "I'll wrap some of these brownies up for you to take with you. I hate to see fresh ones go to waste."

"They'll be going on to my waist, for sure."

"Not if you stay active."

Peri wasn't sure later if it had been the talk with Hayley or the sugar boost from the brownies, but she really did feel more cheerful after she left the farm. Smiling to herself, she pottered around the property and found an ideal location for the tomato plants she wanted to put in.

†

Karla dragged her suitcase into the lift and sighed as the doors closed. Leaving Syd's bed that morning had been hard, but there was the promise of more nights to come.

She was wearing the only clean item of clothing left from the ten days away. The bright floral top, bought at a market stall in Nice, reached down to mid-thigh over her skinny jeans. If she'd had time, she would have dropped her suitcase off at home. Not much point anyway, as Peri wasn't there to do her laundry while she was at work.

There was no one in the reception area when she stepped out of the lift. She'd only taken two steps along the walkway leading to her pod when a voice behind her called out, "Karla, boss man wants to see you."

She turned to see their American intern approaching with two mugs of coffee.

"Can you take these?"

Karla shrugged, indicating her hands were full with the suitcase and her messenger bag.

"No probs. I'll pop those by your desk for you."

They exchanged items, and Karla carried on down the hall. Aldo's space was more like an office than the more open pods the rest of the staff used. He'd sanctioned her holiday, so she didn't think she could be in trouble for taking the time out. Although, he might not be pleased that she'd switched her work phone off for the duration.

He looked up from his screen when she arrived. "Morning. Glad you've come in early."

"Couldn't wait any longer. Missed you, obviously. Bimse Moon, or whatever her name is, gave me these." Karla raised the coffee in her hands.

"Thanks. One's for you. And her name's Luna."

"Right." Karla handed over one of the mugs and sat down in the easy chair next to the desk. "Where's the fire, then?"

"No fire, but we're heading to a hot place. Flight to Albuquerque at noon."

"We? I mean I haven't even been home to unpack."

"Perfect. You're all set then. Passport. Your Esta's still valid."

"Shit, these are the only clean clothes I have."

"Don't worry about that. You can always buy something there. I want our best team on this to finally close out the deal. That's you, Fisbee, and me. Our ride will be here in half an hour, so get that down your neck."

Karla obediently took a sip of the black stuff. How ironic that she'd told Peri she was going to New Mexico.

"I'll fill you in on the details during the trip."

"How long does it take?"

"About eleven hours to Dallas, a two-hour layover, then another hour and half to Albuquerque."

She didn't mind the thought of a long flight in Aldo's company, but Fisbee could be a pain in the arse. If the configuration of seats on the plane allowed, she would opt to sit on her own or next to a stranger. Aldo and Fisbee had known each other since their schooldays at Eton. Fisbee's real name was known only to a select few in the company; he preferred the nickname bestowed on him in prep school. Karla figured she would feel the same if she'd been stuck with something like Erasmus Horatio Kingfisher Fortescue the Third.

They'd probably bonded over their given names. Algernon Donald Ignatius Templeton was clearly destined for great things, in his own mind anyway. He was likely contemplating a knighthood for services rendered in the development of digital resources or some such thing. He often recounted the story of how he'd almost registered the business name as ADIT Solution Services, therefore making an ass out of himself. He could be a bit of an ass at times, but she thought they'd worked well together over the years. They solved other companies' IT problems and took over struggling enterprises, turning them into success stories.

After finishing the coffee, Karla walked back to her pod. Everything was as she'd left it. Aldo had assured her there was nothing that couldn't wait for their return. She booted up her computer anyway to see if there were any emails she should tackle before they left.

She pulled out her phone to call Syd while the machine went through its start-up routine.

"Hey babe, missing me already."

"Yeah. Bad news. My boss has me booked on a flight to Albuquerque today. We'll be away for a week, at least."

"Albuquerque! Isn't that what you told your wife? Am I smashed avocado on toast already?"

"Of course not. Just a weird coincidence."

"Karma, babe. Your lies will come to haunt you."

"Call me Karma Karla."

Syd started to hum the Culture Club anthem, "Karma Chameleon." Karla loved the playful side of her lover and didn't want to destroy the moment by telling her she was heartily sick of hearing that song in relation to her name.

During her high school years, she'd cursed her parents for not spelling her name with a C.

"Very funny." Karla barely managed to keep the sarcasm out of her voice.

Syd stopped humming. "So you're coming back to me? Unless some hot desert chick takes your fancy out there."

"I'd be so lucky. I'll be stuck in a room full of geek boys keen to show off their gaming skills. Like being at a teen techno rally."

"Well, as soon as you're in a private space, give me a ring. Syd's sex line is always open for you."

"Phone sex?"

"Don't tell me you've never had it?"

"I can't say I have. It's never appealed."

"Oh babe. You don't know what you're missing. Syd's silver tongue will have you screaming out her name across the airwaves in no time."

A wave of heat washed through Karla's body. "Syd's silver tongue is already working it's magic. I'll need to hang up now. I can hear my colleagues down the hall."

"Stay wet for me, baby." With those final sultry words, Syd's face disappeared from the screen and Karla squirmed in her seat. It was going to be a long week.

CHAPTER ELEVEN

Peri paced out the area she'd chosen. The greenhouse didn't need to be very big, but she wanted to have somewhere to raise seedlings during the winter months.

"Hello!"

She glanced around to see Hayley approaching quickly.

"Sorry to put this on you, but we have a bit of an emergency at the farm. Would you be okay with picking Bean up from school? Normally she would take the bus and walk up the hill, but she's bringing her art project home and it's too bulky for her to carry." The woman was red in the face and her words came out in a rush.

"Yes, of course. No problem."

"Oh, thank you so much. And if you wouldn't mind keeping her here. I'll let you know when the crisis is over."

"Is everyone okay?"

"Yes. A machinery malfunction, but it needs the three of us to get it sorted. Oh, and do come for tea. Thanks again."

Hayley set off back around the side of the cottage.

"Wait. Hayley. Which school?"

"The one on the main road before the Co-op. They finish in twenty minutes."

Peri heard the roar of the quad bike heading back up to the farm. She wondered why she hadn't heard it arrive. She glanced at her watch. Bean would be standing at the school gates wondering where her ride was if she didn't go now. Martin had been patient, taking Peri out for a few evening sessions in the vehicle. She was more confident about driving on the road but still wanted to trade in the Range Rover for something smaller.

Bean was indeed standing just inside the schoolyard with an adult, when Peri finally arrived. She'd had to park in the community centre car park, as the limited numbers of spaces near the school were already blocked with the vehicles of other parents collecting their children.

"Peri!" Bean shouted her greeting enthusiastically.

The person Peri assumed was a staff member was holding what looked like a large cardboard box and moved forward then.

"Sorry I'm a bit late. I've had to park across the way."

"Just glad you could make it."

Peri carefully took the box from the woman and let Bean lead the way back across the road to the car park. When they reached the Range Rover, Peri stowed the box in the back, and Bean put her backpack next to it.

"Can I take a peek?"

"Sure."

Peri opened the flaps and found she was looking at a complex and detailed diorama of a farm. A number of animals dotted the fields surrounding the house and outbuildings.

"How wonderful. I hope you got good marks for this."

"I won first prize." Bean sounded almost apologetic about winning.

As they drove back along the road, they passed the street leading to the high school. "Would Rory want a lift as well?"

"Oh no. He usually stays in the library until it closes. He either does his homework or works on his novel."

"Have you read any of it?"

"No. He doesn't want anyone to see it until it's finished. He sometimes talks to me about whether or not plot ideas might work. They all sound really good to me."

Back at the cottage, they settled on the patio with a glass of apple juice each.

"Do you think that's a good place for my greenhouse?" Peri pointed to the area she'd staked out.

"I guess so. Better to ask Dad."

"I'm thinking of putting in a pond over there as well."

"Are you going to put fish in it?"

"No. I just thought it could look pretty with some lily pads and maybe attract some frogs."

"Oh, good. 'Cos fish don't last long. Jude's mum bought koi carp for their pond. They didn't last two days before the herons got them."

"I haven't seen any herons."

"There are some that nest further down the river and a heronry up in the hills behind them."

"Heron Ridge. Of course, I should have realised that."

"I hate my name," the girl blurted out.

Peri looked at her wondering what brought that on. "Why?"

"I've always been called Bean at primary school. When I start at the high school in September, I just know the teachers are all going to call me Beatrice. That will be the name on my student record. It totally sucks."

"It's a nice name."

"No it isn't. Sounds sort of old-fashioned. I don't know what my parents were thinking. I don't even have a middle name to fall back on. What's Peri short for?"

"It isn't short for anything. I was christened Pearl. By the time I started school, I refused to answer to it. When I was eighteen, I changed my name by deed poll."

"You can do that?"

"Yes."

"Oh, wow! I could choose my own name?" Bean's whole face lit up at the thought.

"You could." Peri watched Bean's face and wondered at the list of possible names going through the child's mind.

A low flying helicopter disturbed the peace.

Peri glanced up. "What are they looking for?"

"That's an air ambulance. Maybe a rambler stuck on the moors."

"How do you know?"

"By the colour. That one's yellow. The cop ones are black."

They watched it fly across the valley and disappear over the hill.

Peri wondered how much longer she needed to keep Bean with her. She only had water left to offer her and was on the point of saying so. Another loud noise started up. It took Peri a moment to realise it was a ring tone. Bean fished a phone out of her pocket.

"Okay, Mum." She looked at Peri. "You can get rid of me now."

"Hey, you're no trouble."

Before leaving the house, Peri picked up the bag she'd left by the door.

Rory appeared from behind the barn as Peri parked in front of it. "Where did he come from? He didn't pass the cottage."

"Oh no. He walks across the fields. It's a shorter route from the school," Bean replied.

He joined them and peered into the boot Peri had opened. "You've brought it home."

"Yeah. Mum couldn't make it, so Peri came to get me."

Rory lifted the box out. "Thanks, Peri." He set off towards the house.

Peri took her bag out and caught up with Rory before he reached the front door.

"I've brought a couple of books I thought you might like to look at."

He set the box down and looked inside the bag. Stephen King's *On Writing* was on top of the pile. "Oh, wow. My English teacher told me I should read that one."

"Yes, it's very good. You don't need to read it cover to cover. I still find it useful to dip into now and again."

Rory thanked Peri and carried both the bag of books and Bean's art project upstairs.

The meal was delicious, as expected. With everything eaten, Rory and Bean disappeared to their rooms. Adam muttered something about needing to clean some tools in the barn.

Left with the two adults, Peri brought up the subject she'd been thinking about during the night. "I want to sell the Range Rover. I'd prefer something smaller. I thought I'd go to one of the dealerships in Halifax tomorrow."

"Shit, that thing's practically brand new." Martin gave her a quizzical look. "What's the mileage?"

"Just under seven thousand. As far as I know, the longest trips it's done were the ones we made up here."

"God, they'll be paying you." Martin sat back in his chair. "A friend of mine is looking for something like that. He'd pay cash."

"Really. Is he some kind of drug baron?"

Hayley spluttered into her coffee cup.

"No. Just an accountant. You all right, love?" He reached over and patted his wife on the back. She nodded.

"Went down the wrong way."

"What price would you be asking?"

"About half what Karla paid. That will piss her off if she ever finds out."

"Well…" Martin scratched his chin. "I wouldn't tell Phil that. He's a haggler. Quote a bigger price and let him knock you down. He'll drive away happy, thinking he got the better of you."

"You make him sound like a real gent, taking advantage of an old lady."

"Were you planning to buy new?"

"Not necessarily. Second-hand would be fine. It's just for a runabout, but something robust enough to get up the hill in the winter."

"Could try one of the auctions."

"I wouldn't know what to look for. I thought I'd just try one of the local car dealers. They usually have trade-ins, don't they?"

"Yeah, with low mileage. Only driven by an old lady to church on Sundays."

"That works for this old lady."

The full moon lit up the landscape. Peri parked in front of her cottage and stood outside for several minutes. Enjoying this view was one of the things she was learning about country life and the absence of light pollution. She appreciated the cycles of the moon and the brilliance of sunrises and sunsets. Re-familiarising herself with the constellations she could identify was another source of enjoyment.

Settled down for the night and waiting for sleep to come, Peri thought over the events of the day. For the first time since seeing the evidence of Karla's infidelities, she felt she could get through the hurt and fill her life with positive things. She fell asleep thinking about the greenhouse and the plants she would grow.

†

Rory set the book aside and turned out the light. He'd started on the Stephen King one. Peri had chosen well.

Finally, someone he could talk to about writing without feeling embarrassed. He'd always felt like the odd one out in the family. Middle child syndrome was a thing, it seemed, validating his experience. And there was no way he was going to get sucked into taking part in the family business. He didn't mind helping out with the lambing, but if it were up to him, he would close the other operation down. Not that he'd get the chance, with Adam so entrenched in keeping it going.

He sometimes fantasised about making an anonymous call to the cops, but that would bring all sorts of crap down on his parents. He couldn't do that to them.

Closing his eyes to shut out the darkness, he reached down beneath the sheets. The image of the maths teacher bent over the desk at the front of the classroom was all he needed to drive any thoughts of Adam and farm problems out of his mind.

CHAPTER TWELVE

The dry heat sandblasted her face, as she stepped out of the air-conditioned terminal. The pilot had included a weather update in his pre-landing announcements. Ninety degrees on the ground. When Karla translated that into Celsius, it was just over thirty-two. Well out of her comfort zone. She was glad she'd taken Aldo's advice and bought a pair of cargo shorts during their layover in Dallas. Wearing those and a newly acquired Dallas Cowboys ball cap, she thought she would blend in with a good portion of the local population.

After fifteen hours of travel plus the waiting to board at Heathrow, she was hoping for some down time at their hotel. She needed a shower at the very least. It was still daylight in

Albuquerque, but she figured it was about three in the morning at home.

They were barely settled in the taxi when Aldo spoke. "I'm not sure I'll be able to sleep yet. How about we reconvene in the bar in an hour?"

Fisbee grunted in agreement and Karla nodded. Sleeping wasn't an option when the boss made the plans, even if he just needed company while he enjoyed a few beers. They'd taken advantage of the free drink available during their flights, and Karla really didn't want anything else alcoholic. She hoped she could get away with ordering a pitcher of iced tea.

Staying up for the extra few hours hadn't helped restore her sleep pattern. She'd lain awake for several hours, reliving scenes from her time in Monaco with Syd. When she reached the breakfast room at seven thirty the next morning, Fisbee was already seated in front of a plateful of food.

Karla sipped at her orange juice and watched with disgust, as her colleague poured maple syrup over the mound of blueberry pancakes, covering a pile of bacon in the process as well.

"Are you really going to eat all that?"

"Yeah. It's awesome, isn't it?"

"Awesome isn't the word I would use. Heart attack on a plate comes to mind. Syrup and bacon? Yuck."

"I would appreciate it if you didn't make negative comments on my food." He grinned at her before shoving a large forkful of dripping pancake into his mouth.

Not for the first time since joining her colleague in the dining room, Karla wished she'd ordered room service instead. She glanced at her phone. Still no message from Syd in reply to her question about a good time to connect. Out of sight, out of mind. Had her lover moved on to her next conquest already? Karla had no illusions about how faithful Syd would be when she wasn't readily available.

She picked a pineapple chunk out of her fruit salad and slowly chewed.

Aldo gave her outfit the once over when they met in reception. He nodded his approval. As they'd discussed on the plane journey, her role at the first meeting was to appear as his secretary. Put them off guard. The tight sheath dress left nothing to the imagination, and she'd perfected her catwalk prance, hips forward, shoulders back. She would have preferred not to be wearing three-inch stilettos, but they were a necessary part of the costume.

The directors of the company would assume that Aldo had brought her along for a little extra-marital gratification on an otherwise boring business trip. It worked out just as he'd planned. After half an hour of introductions and coffee in the boardroom, they were offered a tour of the facilities. While Aldo and Fisbee went off with the managing director, one of the junior nerds was assigned to showing Karla around. Xander looked about twelve.

The main work areas were open plan, but there were other more private, screened-off spaces, arranged around one of the levels Xander took her to.

"I say. This is so wonderful," she gushed. "It must be marvellous working in this kind of environment."

"Yeah. It is."

"I wonder if I could sit for a moment. These heels are killing me."

"Oh, sure."

Without waiting for him to move, she entered the nearest private work area and sat in the chair in front of the computer. She exhaled an expressive sigh of relief.

"Um, can I get you a drink?"

"That would be lovely. Thank you."

"Coffee, tea, pop?"

"Would you have any iced tea?"

"Yeah. I can get that for you." He walked away, and Karla waited to hear if he'd reached the elevators before making her move. She was about to reach down to her left shoe when he reappeared. Rubbing her leg, she looked up at him questioningly. He held out a magazine.

"I'll need to go down to the fourth-floor kitchen for iced tea. So I thought you might like to look at this while you wait."

It was the same celebrity magazine the hotel had left in the bedroom. "Thank you, again. That's so thoughtful."

He blushed and hurried off.

"Take your time, Xander," she muttered to herself, retrieving the mini pen drive from her shoe's heel.

By the time Xander returned bearing a tray with a tall glass of iced tea, a can of root beer and a selection of biscuits, she was sitting back in the chair, shoes off, seemingly absorbed in a feature on a pop diva she'd never heard of before.

"Oh, you're a star. That looks divine." She sat up and took the drink from the tray.

He set it down on the desk and pulled the tab on the can. "I thought, after you've recovered, we could just go up to the top floor. You get a great view over the city from there."

"I'd like that. Thank you for taking such good care of me."

Karla collapsed onto the sofa in Aldo's room and pulled off her shoes. "I'm not wearing these again." She handed the drive over to her boss.

"No need. Did you have time to download it all?"

"Yeah. I almost feel bad for the little twerp. He was quite sweet."

"Don't go getting sentimental on me, Karla." Aldo booted up his laptop.

"How did you and Fis get on?"

"Pretty good. We've got a better idea of their management structure. But what we've got on here will be pure gold, I hope." He inserted the drive into a USB port.

"It is, trust me. Even captured some of the new coding they're working on for one of their clients."

"Excellent."

"I can't believe they fell for the bimbo trick. Wouldn't they have done any research on us beforehand?"

"It's what we would have done, but these guys are amateurs. There's no way you should have been able to get into this part of their system."

"Very true. Oh, while we were admiring the view from the top floor, Xander had a bit of moan about the current occupant of the White House. Said he's fed up with all the Maga shit."

"Maga?"

"Make America Great Again. What's with the 'again,' he asked? 'America is great.' I was tempted to give him an outsider's perspective, but it would probably have been wasted on him. He did say that if the President wants to send everyone with any Mexican DNA back across the Rio Grande, this place would be a ghost town."

"Of course. That's what's so ironic about this obsession with immigrants here. Everyone in this country came from somewhere else." Aldo looked back at his laptop screen and pumped his fist. "Oh wow. Karla, this is magic."

"Great. Can I go and slip into something more comfortable?"

"Absolutely. I'll send the code stuff over to you. How about we reconvene for dinner about eight and discuss the next steps?"

"I'm good with that. See you later." She picked up her shoes and headed out the door. With any luck, she'd be able to catch up with Syd and have the promised phone sex session.

†

Peri was glad Martin had offered to come with her to look at cars. She wouldn't have known whether or not she was getting a good deal.

On the way to the dealership, Martin filled her in on what to expect. "They'll try to tell you they can't possibly knock anything off the list price, but don't you believe it. You pick out the car you're interested in and then let me do the talking."

Although Peri had thought she would buy a used car, the price Phil had offered for the Range Rover meant she could afford to get a new vehicle and still have a substantial amount left. The display of cars on the forecourt and in the showroom seemed overwhelming at first, but she had done her research and didn't take long to make a decision.

Martin walked around the hatchback she pointed to. "Is it just the colour you like?"

"I'm not a total airhead, Martin. I don't want this colour anyway. They have it in something called eternal blue. I looked it up online. This one fits what I'm looking for…a compact size, but with enough horsepower to make it up the hill. And it's an automatic."

"I wouldn't recommend that myself. You have more control with a manual."

"Yes, but I'm not comfortable with shifting gears, as you know."

The first time Martin had driven with her, the experience left him shaking. Although they had only gone a few miles, he insisted on driving them back. She was surprised when he offered to take her out again a few days later. She had improved with his gentle tuition.

A salesman approached and addressed Martin. "Can I help you folks?"

As they'd agreed, Martin did the negotiating. When they walked off the lot, she was committed to buying the car even though delivery time for the colour she wanted was three weeks.

"Are you okay with waiting that long?" Martin asked when they'd driven away. "Phil's collecting the Range Rover from you on Friday, isn't he?"

"Yes. I'll be carless for a few weeks but I'm okay with that. There's the work to do on the greenhouse and the pond."

"Well, if you need anything from the shops, just let us know. Hayley can pick things up for you when she does her egg deliveries."

"That's very kind. I might take her up on that."

Back at the cottage, Martin looked at the space she'd marked out for the greenhouse.

"Yes, that'll work. When do you want to get started?"

"The glass panels are arriving the day after tomorrow."

"Good. I'll bring the wood I told you about. There's enough for the shelving and counter space you'll need."

"You've done so much for me already. I don't know how I can repay you, as you've refused any offer of money. I'll be forever in your debt."

"It's enough for us to know we have a good neighbour. We weren't looking forward to Sheepfold being used as a holiday let."

She watched him drive up the track to the farm and turned back into the house to make the next important decision of the day, what to have for lunch.

†

Lying back on the hotel bed, Karla positioned the phone where Syd wanted it. *FaceTime is turning into something else.* Syd's disembodied voice continued its instructions, sounding muted between Karla's legs.

"Start slowly, one finger, then two. In and out. Yes, perfect. Keep up that rhythm."

Karla moaned softly, as her fingers moved in the delicate, wet folds.

"Louder. I need to hear you coming."

"I don't think I can."

"You can. You will." Syd's voice took on a deeper, huskier tone. "Come on, baby. Keep stroking. Add another finger. I want to see your juices flowing over your hand."

Karla cried out as the third finger hit the sensitive spot.

"That's the way. I know you can do this. Keep going."

When she came, flooding the sheets, Karla screamed out Syd's name.

"Good work, baby."

Karla raised her hips to remove her hand.

"No!" Syd's shout reverberated around the room. "I didn't tell you to stop, did I? Get back in position. You'll keep coming until I say you're finished. Is that clear?"

"Yes." Karla settled back down on the bed.

"Get the phone back in position. Now!"

Karla obeyed and waited.

"You've earned yourself a spanking next time I see you. Now, let's start again."

Karla squirmed. Just the suggestion of receiving a spanking from Syd brought another rush of liquid from her centre.

By the time the call ended, she was lying in a puddle of her own making, surrounded by an overwhelming musky scent and shaking from the intensity of the final orgasm. Reaching between her legs, she hoped her phone had survived the soaking.

CHAPTER THIRTEEN

Exhausted to the point of falling asleep in the taxi, Karla dragged herself up the path to the front door. Once inside, she dropped her case in the hallway. Too bad Peri wasn't there to do her laundry; she wasn't in any state to start fiddling around with the washing machine. They'd drunk far too much on the plane. Aldo didn't let up. An almost continuous flow of gin and tonics had followed the two initial bottles of champagne.

Taking a shower might have helped revive her, but after removing her clothes, she fell back onto the bed and crashed.

She woke in the middle of the night with a splitting headache and her mouth so dry she could still be breathing in desert sand. After a long hot shower and swallowing a gallon of tap water, Karla started to feel more alive. Again, she missed Peri's presence. The coffee pot would be brewing, made to the strength she liked.

A scan of the kitchen counter revealed the absence of the state-of-the-art Krups Espresso machine. She was sure Peri had left it, saying she was happy to make do with filter coffee at the cottage. Karla surveyed the kitchen. The toaster oven was missing too. They had argued back and forth about that, before Peri agreed to let it stay for the time being.

The refrigerator shelves were empty. Probably a good thing, as she had been away for three weeks. There had been a bottle of Sauvignon Blanc, not that she wanted an alcoholic drink of any description right then, but it couldn't have walked out by itself.

Has Peri been here?

In a sudden panic, Karla walked into the living room and flicked on the overhead light. "Shit!"

She paced around the now more open area and inventoried the missing items…coffee table, side tables, lamp, rug, Peri's favourite recliner, and two empty spaces on the walls.

"What the fuck?"

Her headache returned full force, as she ran up the stairs to her office. A ring of dust on her desk highlighted where the printer had been. "No, no, no!" She reached down and opened the bottom drawer of the desk and heaved a sigh of relief. The phones were still there. All seven of them. She counted twice. Her secrets were safe.

What had prompted this? She'd covered her tracks well. Peri had never suspected anything before. Karla pulled out her phone. It was only four in the morning. Even if Peri answered, it wasn't going to be a good time to confront her.

At least two hours before the nearest coffee shop opened, she might as well get the laundry started and check the post. Downstairs, she poured herself another pint glass of water and drank it down before retrieving her suitcase from the hall. Now that she was more alert than she had been the night before, she saw the stack of mail placed neatly on the hat stand and another against the wall by the door. She scooped it up and carried the whole lot back into the living room. She sat down on the sofa to begin sorting.

Most of it was for Peri. Karla had told her she should redirect her mail, but Peri hadn't been sure the post office delivered to the cottage. She said Karla could bring anything with her at the weekend.

One large manilla envelope had no post mark and only her name on it, handwritten.

Karla opened the flap and pulled out the official-looking letter. It took her a few moments to process what she was reading. When it did register, she couldn't believe it. Peri was filing for divorce.

The lawyer's name rang a bell. Sharon Greenbaum. Wasn't she the bitch hooked up with Peri's bestie, Dana? They must have put Peri up to it. No way her wife would have thought of doing anything like this on her own.

Karla sat back and closed her eyes. There was no other option. She'd have to face Peri in person, explain that whatever she thought was going on was a one off, an aberration. It wouldn't happen again. What did Peri think she'd done? What did she know?

By six o'clock, she'd put two loads of washing on, answered all her emails, and drunk two more pints of water.

The pounding in her head had lessened. The short walk to the coffee shop and back helped to invigorate her further. After a good hit of caffeine and a bacon sandwich, she was ready to take the next step. Aldo had told her to take two days off, so a drive up to Yorkshire was on the cards.

She opened the garage and stared open-mouthed into yet another empty space. The car wasn't there. Her pride and joy.

"Unfuckingbelievable! She doesn't even drive!"

She walked out, leaving the door open. Back in the house she paced around, wondering what else she'd missed. Remembering the missing wine bottle from the fridge, she opened the drinks cupboard in the kitchen.

The whisky bottles were gone, but she'd left the gin. How thoughtful! Only then did she look over at the wall behind the door and see that the wine rack was empty.

She found just one nearby car hire company open early. The best they could offer was a five-year-old Ford Escort. Karla didn't have time to shop around. It was after ten by the time she drove away, and she immediately encountered a tailback on the M25. By lunchtime, she'd only reached Watford Gap Services and passed the last of the *To the North* motorway signs. According to the satnav app on her phone, there was another two and half hours' drive time before she'd reach her destination. Another hit of coffee and a sandwich, and she was on her way again. Each mile closer only spurred on her anger.

CHAPTER FOURTEEN

The sound of a car engine stopping outside the cottage caught Peri's attention. She was expecting Martin and Adam to arrive with the building supplies for the greenhouse, but it didn't sound like the farm truck.

She reached the door at the same time as her visitor and came face to face with Karla.

"We need to talk."

"I don't think so."

"You can't just take everything away and expect me to sit back and say nothing."

"I thought the documents Sharon left for you made it clear that any communication would be through our respective divorce lawyers."

"Please, Peri. At least give me a chance to explain. I've driven all this way."

Peri stepped outside and closed the door behind her, forcing Karla to move back. "Explain what? How you've been lying to me all these years? If you're going to tell me that Sydney Louisa Devereaux is your first and only fling, you can save your breath."

Karla looked shocked. "How did you know...?"

"I may not be on social media myself, but people I know are. Miss Devereaux has a high profile. I know about some of your other liaisons, because I found your phones."

"What? But..."

"Yes. I put them back where they were, but only after retrieving the reams of text messages to all those women. I expect they weren't the only ones." Peri wasn't going to reveal Dana and Sharon's involvement in gaining the information. She wasn't giving Karla any ammunition to use against her in the divorce proceedings.

"I want the car back. You can't even drive."

"Actually, I can. I've had a valid driver's licence since I was eighteen. Just never had the need for a car before. Thank you for putting the documents in my name."

"That was for tax purposes, and you know it."

"I guess you'll just have to buy a new one."

"You won't get away with this."

"Oh, I think I will. Now, why don't you piss off back to your love nest?"

Karla shook her head and walked over to the open garage. "Where is it? Just give me the keys. I can get the ownership changed."

"Too late. I sold it."

"What? No way!"

"Yes. The new owner is over the moon, especially as he got it at a bargain rate."

"Fuck. It's hardly broken in. You could still have asked top price." Karla paced back to Peri. "At least you can give me what you got for it."

"I don't think so. I consider it payment in part for twenty years of skivvying for you. That's all I ever was, right? A live-in housekeeper. And I've spent the money, some of it anyway, on a new car. I'm taking delivery next week."

Peri knew the signs. Karla was working herself up into a full-blown rage. Whether or not she would have lashed out, her momentum was halted by the sound of a vehicle turning in at the gate.

The farm truck pulled up to a noisy stop in front of the cottage. Martin jumped out of the passenger side and greeted Peri cheerfully.

"Morning. All set to get started?"

Adam had climbed out of the driver's seat and stood with his mouth open. Peri was amused to see his blatant reaction to Karla's good looks.

"Yes. Karla's just leaving."

"You haven't heard the last of this." She stomped off to her rental car. The slammed door and a clashing of gears, before she managed to get it into reverse, disturbed the morning's peace. At the gate, Karla stopped to toss something out the window.

Peri breathed a sigh of relief, as the car disappeared down the lane.

"That was Karla? Wow!" Martin looked as impressed as his son.

"Don't tell me. You expect all lesbians to wear dungarees and DMs and look like the back end of a bus."

Martin had the grace to look sheepish. "Not exactly. But okay, maybe a bit." He looked over at his son. "Put your tongue back in your head and start unloading." He grabbed a shovel from the back of the truck. "Come on, Peri. Show me where you want to put this."

"I'll just pick up what she threw out. It looks like some post from the London house. The space for the greenhouse is marked out."

†

Reaching the main road, Karla sped back the way she'd come. If she stepped on it, she could be back in London in time to meet up with Syd. She was in desperate need of relief from the tension knotting her neck and shoulders, along with the burgeoning headache. A night of passion with her lover would help erase some of that.

A flash in her rearview mirror alerted her, too late, to the speed camera. She glanced at her speedometer and groaned. That was going to be a four pointer at least. Added to the points she'd already accumulated, she would lucky to still be holding a driver's licence by Christmas.

How did she not know that Peri was a licensed driver? She had never shown any interest in driving the car. And how did she get the info off her phones? She wasn't that technically adept. Karla knew she should have ditched the phones. It wasn't like she was going to call any of the women again. Well, maybe Marli, when Syd eventually tired of her. She had that sexy Swedish accent and an unapologetic enthusiasm for exploring each other's bodies. Or perhaps Lacey. Brighton was an easy drive down to the coast, one of her favourite hunting grounds.

When Syd tired of her... Karla expected that would happen some time, hopefully not for a long while yet. Karla returned the hire car and rushed home for a quick shower and change.

A delay on the Underground did nothing to improve her mood. It was after ten by the time she reached Syd's penthouse pad near Regent's Park. As soon as Syd opened the door, Karla launched into a description of her day, finishing up with the question that had been bothering her since early morning.

"How did she find out about you? I only posted a few pics on Facebook. She doesn't do social media of any kind."

"Someone she knows must have seen it. That's the problem. You don't know who's connected. A friend of a friend could be on your friends list."

"Shit, shit, shit! She's cleaned me out. I paid for the cottage, the car, the vintage whisky and wines. The original paintings in the living room."

"Nothing that can't be replaced, apart from the cottage, but you didn't want to live there anyway. Let her have the divorce, then you're free. No strings."

"I know. Divorce was my ultimate goal, but not like this."

Syd tweaked a nipple, eliciting a moan from Karla. "You're still far too wound up. I think you need some intensive therapy." She stripped away Karla's top, then lowered her mouth onto the nearest breast and sucked hard.

Karla didn't think her body would respond, but it did. By the time they moved into the bedroom, her clit was throbbing with the raw need Syd always managed to awaken.

CHAPTER FIFTEEN

The work on the garden was going well, with help from Adam and Martin. The greenhouse hadn't taken long to put up. They started digging out the pond the next morning. Martin went back to the farm to fetch a wheelbarrow. Adam had barely ever looked at Peri, just kept his head down and did whatever his dad told him.

"What's your problem, Adam?" Peri asked, when she heard the farm truck drive off.

"Bean," he grunted forcefully. "I don't think she should be spending time here."

Peri studied the closed-in look she'd frequently observed on Adam's face. "Are you for real? You think I'm corrupting your little sister? I'm surprised at you, Adam. Do you really subscribe to the view promoted by the tabloids that all homosexuals are paedophiles?"

He looked away from her, unable to meet her eyes.

"That is what you think, isn't it? Well, for your information, most offenders are straight males. I'm not interested in little girls. I'm old enough to be Bean's grandma. The only female in your family at risk from my attentions would be your mother, and even she is a bit young for me."

He grunted.

"I'm a novelty round here. Bean's interest in visiting me will wane eventually. Especially when she starts high school."

Martin came round the side of the house pushing the wheelbarrow. "You two slacking? I leave you alone for five minutes, and you think you can stop and stare at the view. This earth isn't going to move itself."

"Slave driver. Come on, Adam. Let's fill this barrow."

To her relief, the boy did look at her then. For the first time that morning, the smile reached his eyes. "Okay."

They were packing up for the day, when the sound of a helicopter caught her ears. She looked around to see where it was coming from. Martin and Adam both stood stock still staring up at the sky. With a quickness of movement Peri rarely saw in him, Martin whipped out his phone, punching in a contact.

"Incoming," was all he said before ending the call and slipping the phone back into his pocket. "Wish they wouldn't fly so low. It's really annoying at lambing time. We've got a lot on our hands then, keeping new mums and their offspring fed and watered."

"What's it doing?" Peri asked. "That looks like a police one. I've heard them flying over quite a lot recently."

"Training exercises, mainly. Other times, they're looking for thieves on the run."

"I didn't think there was much crime around here."

"You'd be surprised. Farm equipment is a popular target. Fortunately, they don't usually make it up here. Too much effort."

"Looks like they're away over to Haworth." Adam turned his attention back to the soil he'd been digging out. Martin joined him.

"I heard someone talking about coping stones being lifted from a length of wall along one of the roads near here. Why would anyone do that?"

"They just don't make them like that anymore. There is a market for them." Martin had relaxed back into his usual manner and seemed relieved at the change of subject.

Peri glanced over at the pile of stones they'd brought from the farm to edge the pond and raised an eyebrow.

Martin caught the look and laughed. "No, we've not been out nicking those. They're from our own walls. We had to create a sheep-creep between fields for the sheep movements."

"Sheep-creep?"

"Yes, it's a gap in the wall so the sheep can go into another field without us having to shepherd them."

"I guess I have a lot to learn still about country living."

After they'd gone, refusing the offer of more beer, Peri luxuriated in the bath and scrubbed the dirt from under her fingernails. Waste of time really, as she would be doing more gardening in the morning. She planned to get the tomato plants situated along the south-facing wall of the cottage. Hayley advised her that would be the best place for them.

The sun was setting over the hills at the far end of the valley. Peri relaxed in her favourite recliner and thought back over her day. Seeing Karla had brought up emotions she'd managed to tamp down while working with Martin and Adam.

What would she have been doing today? A Thursday, any Thursday. After coffee and toast, she would have checked her emails. If she were working on a book, she would edit for the first part of the morning. She'd probably put on a load of washing before starting.

Mid-morning was when she would walk to the coffee shop and treat herself to a cappuccino. Time to sit in a corner seat, make a grocery list, think of food Karla liked, some treats for the weekend. Maybe also consider when to book the painter to give the house a freshen up, working out how long it had been since they last decorated. The oven would need cleaning, but she would put that task off as long as she could bear it.

Home and time to fold the laundry before having a bite to eat for lunch. Smoothing out the creases in Karla's tailored jeans. There wasn't much ironing some weeks. Karla didn't often have to wear power suits. She did like cotton shirts though, which were hard to iron and not leave any telltale creases.

Mondays, Wednesdays, and Fridays were Peri's swimming days. The only exercise she took, apart from housework and walking to the shops.

Her life had never felt like a chore, like she was tied to a routine. She loved being the homemaker and welcoming Karla home at the end of her work day, the hunter returned. When had she turned into Karla's mother and not her lover? Sixty is the new forty, so they say now. What age did that make Karla? About twenty-five, the age she was when they first met.

The next morning, Peri went up to the farm for a cuppa and got talking about Karla. Hayley asked the usual question ...how did you meet? Perhaps she thought lesbians had different ways of meeting potential lovers than male/female couples.

Karla had come to Peri's office to install new software. She'd spent the afternoon showing Peri how to get started. A few days later, Peri phoned to ask if she could come back and resolve some trouble with the printer settings. It was just an excuse to see her again. She gathered the courage to ask Karla out to dinner.

"I was flattered when she said yes. I should have known. She was looking for security. When her parents split up, she was shuffled between the two. Then her mother moved back to Spain and took the younger brother with her. Karla and her sister stayed to finish school. With hindsight, it seems obvious I was a safe haven. At first, I couldn't believe she wanted to be with me. With her looks, she could have had anyone. Well, now I know she has been having anyone.

"How long has she been laughing at me? Enjoying the benefits of coming home to cooked meals, a clean house, and a warm body in bed. I never questioned the late nights, the days and sometimes weeks away. It was all part of her job. Her salary increasing year on year kept us in a style of living that was the envy of our friends."

Hayley had listened and nodded her head in sympathy, then asked about Peri's family. That was another story Peri didn't want to dwell on too much.

Turning the corner into the street where she had grown up, Peri noticed the hedge had grown a few more feet in the three years she'd been away and didn't look like it had been pruned or shaped for some time. It wasn't like her father to let it go. He was proud of his garden. The absence of any Christmas lights was odd.

SOLD

The label was plastered over a For Sale sign attached to a wooden post by the hedge. Peri stood on the path, not needing to approach the front door to know that no one was home. The curtainless windows stared blankly back at her.

Next door blazed brightly with a row of lights around the eaves and a decorated tree in full view in their living room window. Peri walked up the path and knocked on the door. She didn't know if they would remember her, or even if they were the same neighbours who had been there while she was living at home.

The woman who answered didn't seem surprised to see her. "Peri. Hello. I wondered if you would be coming by."

"I'm sorry to bother you."

"Do come in."

Peri stepped inside, glad of the warmth.

"Come on through. You look frozen."

Peri followed her into the kitchen. A dozen mince pies were cooling on a rack by the oven.

"I was just about to warm up some mulled wine. Can I tempt you to a glass?"

"Yes, please. Thank you." Peri searched her memory for the woman's name. Lesley, Wendy…

Seated at the table and warmed by the first mouthful of wine and half-eaten mince pie, Peri felt able to ask, "My parents…how long…?"

"Only last week. They've gone to Canada to join your brother and his wife. They've been planning it for some time, once they knew the grandchild was on its way."

"It had always been on the cards, once Rick announced that he wasn't coming home from his gap year. He'd met and married a local girl."

Hayley looked shocked when she finished. "They up and left without telling you?"

"It wasn't really a surprise. They cut me off when I came out to them after university. I might never have known they'd moved, if I hadn't decided to give them another chance that Christmas. They'd left a suitcase with the neighbour, containing the few things I'd left behind when they kicked me out."

"That's awful. I can't imagine abandoning any of my children."

"I was a sinner in the eyes of their God. My mother, particularly, was a strong believer. I think my dad just went along to keep the peace. By the time I was fourteen, I'd stopped going to church. I preferred to spend my Sunday mornings in bed. Rick played the part of the perfect son. He was in the choir. Sang like an angel until his voice broke."

"And you still have no contact with them?"

"No. I used to send Christmas cards, but nothing ever came back. I don't know if they're still alive, or if I have more than one niece or nephew."

"Oh, Peri. That's so sad."

Peri picked at the crumbs on her plate. She hadn't meant to eat another brownie, but they did taste good. Although she wasn't sure about the green bits she had to pick out of her teeth.

"Well, at least, I have the family I choose and who choose me. Thank you for being here." She reached out and grasped Hayley's hand, suddenly filled with a surge of happiness.

Buoyed by the sense of wellbeing, Peri decided it was time to deal with a task she'd been putting off. She returned to the cottage and brought the last cardboard box down from the guest room where she'd been storing it.

Lighting a fire in June didn't seem right. However, it was the best way she could think of to dispose of the box's contents. She knelt in front of the fireplace and lifted out the first batch of cards. Karla had never missed birthdays, Christmas, or their wedding anniversary. Peri forgave her occasional lapses on Valentine's Day, thinking of it as a day that mainly benefitted makers of cards with sickly-sweet sentimental messages.

The first batch of cards went up in flames. A twinge of sadness passed quickly, and she didn't hesitate to consign the rest of the box's contents to a fiery end.

CHAPTER SIXTEEN

Peri stood by the patio doors and surveyed her domain. It was all coming along nicely. Adam had finished the edging around the pond. The natural stonework added a classy dimension.

Hayley had taken her to the garden centre earlier in the week, to advise her on what she needed to set up the greenhouse and the vegetable garden. The tomato plants were in place, so that was one job done.

A blur of movement caught her eye. She stayed by the doors, transfixed as a heron landed gracefully on one of the stones. The regal bird peered into the water, catching its own reflection. Peri knew if she moved it would fly off. She wished her phone wasn't lying on the kitchen counter. There wasn't much likelihood of the heron coming back when it saw there were no fish.

It was worth a try though. Backing away slowly, she retrieved her phone and was able to take a photo before it noticed her and flew away. Deciding that was a sign for her to get moving herself, Peri opened the doors and stepped out into the cool morning air.

After a few hours she was satisfied with the work completed in the greenhouse. The seedlings were planted in trays and arranged on the shelving Martin had constructed, best placed to catch the morning light.

Time for another coffee and one of Hayley's delicious brownies. She'd brought a few down when delivering the eggs earlier. Peri's phone rang before she had time to sit down with the fresh brew. She smiled when she saw it was Dana calling.

"How's it going in lesbo-land?" Typical Dana greeting. No hello, or how are you.

"Pretty good. The greenhouse is up and running. Pond's looking great. I had a visit from a heron this morning. And I can pick up my new car tomorrow."

"Wow. Not just sitting around contemplating your navel, then?"

"No time for that. The weather's been so good, I'm doing my editing work in the evenings. How about you? Dare I ask how the new novel's coming along?"

"You can ask. Bit slow at the moment. Mushy middle. I miss our Wednesday chats."

"I'm here, anytime you want to talk."

"I know. Anyway, how would you feel about a visit this weekend?"

"You're welcome anytime. That would be fantastic."

"Okay. Sharon's taking Friday off, so we can be there by lunchtime."

"Doesn't she usually spend Friday evenings with her family?"

"Yes, but her dad's come down with flu and Levi and Ruth have taken their kids to a Center Parc for the weekend." Dana laughed. "Rather them than me. Oh, and we're bringing food."

"Let me guess. Sharon's not passing Watford Gap before she finds a Waitrose."

"Spot on."

Ending the call with a smile on her face, Peri picked up a brownie and bit off one end. A double hit of coffee and chocolate, and she was ready to tackle some serious gardening in the vegetable patch. She hummed to herself as she dug over a section of soil, and didn't hear the person approach.

A shadow fell across her line of vision, and she turned to find herself face to face with a larger-than-life policeman.

"Morning."

"Oh, hello. I didn't hear you arrive."

"I knocked at the door, but then I thought it was worth checking out here. Sergeant Knowles, at your service."

"Peri. Peri Sanderson."

"Do you mind if I have a look in your greenhouse?"

"Not at all. I've just been potting some seedlings."

"Right." He walked over and looked inside.

Peri followed and watched him poke one of the trays. "Can I ask what you're looking for?"

"One of our helicopter pilots mentioned a new greenhouse when he flew over the valley yesterday. Just checking you're not setting up a marijuana farm."

Peri laughed. "Gosh. I hadn't even thought of that. I bought all this from the local garden centre. I still have the receipt if you want to check."

His smile reached his eyes this time. "I'm sure you're legit. This area does have a certain reputation for growing the stuff. They all think they're related to King David around here and can get away with hiding in the hills."

"King David?"

"King of the Coiners. Local history. Look him up and you'll get what I mean."

"Would you like a coffee? The kettle is still warm."

"Thanks, but I'd better move on. Only really came up to grab a batch of Hayley's brownies. Not worth my life to go back to the station without them."

"You know the Rushfords well?"

"Yes. We were at school together." He tipped his hat to her. "Take care, Ms Sanderson."

Peri walked around the side of the cottage and watched the officer get in his car and continue up the track to the farm. She wandered into the kitchen and eyed the brownies on the plate.

Those bits of greenery she'd thought were some type of herb, could they be marijuana? She had no experience with drugs of any kind. Had Hayley been feeding her hash brownies? It was unthinkable she would do such a thing without telling her.

She waited until she saw the police car drive back down the track, before setting off up the hill carrying the plate.

Hayley saw her approaching from the kitchen window and waved. Peri marched into the house and went straight onto the attack. "Why didn't you warn me?" She thumped the plate down on the table. "I don't do drugs."

"I'm sorry. I...well, you were so down, and they were there. I just wanted to cheer you up."

"A glass of wine would have done the job. I still wouldn't have a clue if that cop hadn't stopped by to see if I was growing weed in my greenhouse."

"Oh."

"Does he know? Or does he turn a blind eye because you're old school pals? Does he take these back to the station and they all sit around giggling?"

"No. I do a separate batch for him...and the kids...obviously. Look, please sit down, Peri. I'll try to explain."

"Explain what, that this nice family I'm living next door to is really a gang of drug dealers?"

"Hardly that. We only supply friends who use it to relieve medical conditions."

"I'm sure that will stand up well in court." Peri didn't give Hayley a chance to reply. She marched out and half walked, half ran back to the cottage.

She rooted out the bottle of Glenfiddich she'd been saving for a special occasion and poured two fingers into a glass. This was her drug of choice, when needed. She had to admit, single malt didn't give her the same buzz of euphoria the brownies did.

She thought she'd only closed her eyes for a minute, when a tapping on the patio doors brought her fully awake. Peri blinked. Martin was standing outside.

He came in and seated himself on the sofa. "Hayley's told me what she did, and she is truly sorry. She didn't mean any harm."

"I know that." Peri pulled herself up. She hoped she hadn't been snoring with her mouth open when Martin arrived. "It does worry me that I'm living next to a cannabis farm, if that's the right term. What if you go to jail? What happens to the kids? Do they know about it?"

"They know. And they know not to talk about it to their friends. And Hayley's mum would look after Rory and Bean." He gazed out at the garden. "Look, it's been a family business since my dad set it up in the sixties. It's not a big operation. We only ever have a dozen plants growing in a well-concealed shed, built much like a bomb shelter."

Peri held up her hands. "I don't want to know any more. Best not to, if I'm ever questioned. But I'm guessing it has to be ventilated. Wouldn't the smell give it away?"

Martin smiled. "We don't get any stray ramblers up here, and it doesn't bother the sheep." He spread his hands in a placating gesture. "Look, we're not drug dealers. We don't sell to kids. It's just for friends who use it recreationally or for medical reasons. The money we make from it is fairly minimal, donations really. It's set aside for university funding for Rory and possibly Bean, if she wants to go the academic route."

"That's all very commendable, Martin. But if you're growing and selling the stuff, even if it's only to friends, that does make you a drug dealer. Your friend Phil, is he involved?" Peri remembered her suspicions about the accountant's payment in cash for the Range Rover.

"Indirectly, you could say. His wife's a district nurse. She lets us know about people who are struggling with pain relief through the usual routes...painkillers, alcohol. If a few spliffs helps them get through the night, what's the harm?"

"And the brownies?"

"They're for folks who don't smoke or have given up." Martin stood. "Look, I'm sorry. This has obviously been a shock for you. I can't change the way you feel about it. I'm sorry you found out the way you did. You might want to think on it though. It's a different culture here than what you were used to in London."

He walked back out through the patio doors. Peri couldn't decide whether or not there was a hidden threat in his parting words.

After a few minutes, she got up and went into the kitchen to make a cheese sandwich. She ate it sitting on the patio. The combination of the whisky and the nap had left her fuzzyheaded. She didn't feel any more comfortable with the situation, and she was glad her friends were coming up for the weekend.

The next morning, she almost tripped over the egg box left at the front door. She was glad Hayley hadn't knocked as usual. Peri wasn't ready for another confrontation. Clearly, her neighbour wasn't either. She thought about taking the eggs back. The idea of having two fresh ones for breakfast won that argument in her head. Still, the idea of Hayley delivering her special, weed-infested brownies with her eggs didn't sit well.

Peri managed to put the drug business out of her mind during the morning, while she worked on edits for an action-adventure novel. The baddies in the story were involved in gunrunning, not drugs, for which she was grateful. The car was delivered just as she was thinking of stopping for lunch. She sat in it for a while, savouring the new car smell, before driving it carefully into the garage. There would be time to take it out for a drive after the visit from her friends.

The afternoon passed peacefully. After setting out some transplants in the garden, Peri felt she'd earned a rest. She settled on the patio with a glass of beer to enjoy seeing how far the garden had come along.

She didn't know she'd drifted off, until a wet nose nudged her leg. Radar stared up at her, tongue lolling and tail wagging. Bean wasn't far behind and stood hesitantly on the other side of the table. It took a moment for Peri to see that she was holding a small, wriggling creature.

Peri smiled at the girl. Whatever she thought of the parents' activities, she couldn't take it out on the youngster.

Encouraged, Bean approached and placed the kitten on her lap. "This is the one you wanted, isn't it? They've been weaned now."

Wide-open green eyes gazed around, and small paws kneaded Peri's legs, before the fur ball settled with a tiny purring noise. Peri stroked its head. "Yes, this was the one."

Bean had taken her to see the litter on her second visit to the farm, and she'd immediately picked out the only ginger kitten of the six.

"He's already quite adventurous. Mum says you might want to have him neutered when he's older, or you'll never know where he gets to at night."

Peri wanted to say she couldn't accept the kitten, yet another tie to the family. Looking at Bean's beaming face, she couldn't bring herself to disappoint her. She had said she would like one of the kittens. She was doing them a favour, really, as they needed to find homes for all of them. She stroked the kitten's small head again.

"Does he have a name?"

"Oh no. We don't give them names unless we're keeping them ourselves."

"I don't have any experience naming pets. Do you have any ideas?"

"Hm. I think he's going to be a big explorer." She scratched her chin thoughtfully. "He looks like a Jasper."

"Jasper." Peri tried the name out. "Yes, I like it. Thank you, Bean."

"Oh, Mum thought you would need these to start off with, if you can't get into town today." Bean drew a bag out of her backpack. "Don't give him milk to drink. Cow's milk is definitely a no-no. It gives cats the runs."

"I didn't know that." Peri looked at the bag of dry brown pellets. "Is that all he can eat? It doesn't look very appetising."

"Mix it with some water for now. In a week or so, he'll be okay with tinned food. You should start off with a little mixed in with this."

"You must be an expert. I'll come to you if I have any problems."

Radar finished his inspection of the pond and came back to gaze at the kitten settled on Peri's lap. She reached over and stroked his head. "Sorry, Radar. You're still my favourite dog."

"He likes the kittens. When their mamma goes hunting, he watches them for her."

"Do I need to keep Jasper indoors? Will he try to get back to the farm?"

"He's not likely to get far yet. Should be okay outside as long as you keep an eye on him."

"Okay. Let's see how he does." She set Jasper down on the patio. He opened his eyes and wobbled onto his feet. Radar lay down so that their noses were level, placing his paws protectively on either side of the kitten.

"That's amazing. I've never seen that before."

"Radar thinks he's the dad."

By the time Bean and Radar left, half an hour later, Jasper had ventured onto the grass and made it as far as the pond. Peri watched anxiously in case he fell in, but he just sniffed around the edges.

†

Who knew so much fun could be had with a ball of string and a kitten? Peri didn't get back to any of her garden planting until midafternoon. Jasper, tired out from chasing string and anything else that moved, was fast asleep on a patio chair. She thought he would be safe there as he wouldn't be able to climb down on his own.

She was just thinking of stopping for a cool drink, when a voice hailed her from the other side of the boundary wall.

Rory had removed his uniform tie, and his shirt was hanging out. The blazer was slung over his backpack. Usually, he'd be neatly dressed. Peri thought the school should have a summer uniform when the days were so hot. There was a campaign in the town to relax the rules, so boys could wear shorts. The girls had the option of wearing skirts. She supposed the boys should be given that option too.

"Hi. I'm going to get a cold drink. Would you like something?"

He nodded and stepped easily over the three-foot high wall. When she came back with a glass of lemonade for each of them, he had Jasper in his lap, a contented purr coming from the small creature.

"Bean brought him over earlier. Shouldn't she have been in school as well?"

"No. They had a teacher training day."

They sipped their drinks in companionable silence. Peri had experienced this before with Rory on previous visits. He didn't seem to feel the need to fill silences with words. Bean was quite the chatterbox by comparison. Rory didn't speak again until he'd emptied the glass and put it on the table.

"Thanks for that. Look, I know Mum screwed up, giving you some of her special brownies."

"You know about that?"

"Yeah, I heard Mum and Dad talking about it. They're worried you might dob them in."

"Dob them in?"

"Grass them up. You know, tell the cops."

Peri sighed and gazed over the peaceful scene in front of her. "I don't have any experience with drugs of any kind, apart from prescriptions for antibiotics on occasion. It was a shock for me to learn about your family's extraneous farming activity. The revelation came right after a visit from a policeman, who wanted to check out my new greenhouse. I love this place, and your family has been very kind to me. I wouldn't like to think they've given me all this help with things to keep me sweet."

Rory sat up straight, and Jasper mewled at the change in position. "No. That's not how they are. When they found out you'd be living on your own here, Mum and Dad just wanted to make sure you'd be all right."

"You're not worried about the operation being discovered? Your parents going to jail?"

"No. I do worry a bit about Adam. I think he's supplying some of his friends. He could get caught dealing."

Peri finished her lemonade and set the glass down. She could do with a stronger drink. The thought occurred to her that she didn't have the right to judge anyone else's chosen drug, if she was dependent on alcohol to solve her problems.

"What do you think of the garden? I've got most of the planting done now." She stood and walked over to the vegetable patch. Rory followed, still holding onto Jasper.

"You'll need to protect them from slugs. As soon as we get some rain they'll be out in force."

"Oh. How do I do that?"

"Crushed eggshells are good to put around seedlings. Make sure they're dry before crushing them. If you don't mind wasting beer, then you can set traps for them. Mum uses plastic bottles. Cut both ends off, stick one end in the ground and fill it up. Seems they like a drink but it kills them."

She looked at Rory's serious face. "How do you know all that? I didn't think you were interested in outdoor things."

"Osmosis. Growing up on a farm..." his voice tailed off.

"You don't want to be a farmer though."

"No, it bores me rigid. I'm sure I'm a disappointment to Dad, but he's got Adam trained up to follow on with the family tradition."

Peri sighed. The family tradition. They were back to that, and it wasn't a subject she wanted to pursue further just then.

Peri found it hard to settle to anything after Rory left. She watched the kitten exploring his new territory. She was careful not to let him roam out of her line of sight. Finally, she scooped him up and went into the kitchen. She put Jasper on the floor by his water bowl. He lapped some up, while she poured herself a beer. She prepared some of the unappetising kibble and put the dish by his head. He munched away happily.

Thoughts swirled around in her mind. Had Hayley sent Bean with the kitten to soften her up? The timing seemed suspicious. Had she and Martin prompted Rory to pay her a visit as well? He had stopped by a few times to talk about writing and books. Not surprising, Adam hadn't turned up as well. He was clearly the weak link. If his brother knew he was dealing, who else knew?

Somehow, she got through the evening between watching video clips of *The L Word* on YouTube and playing with Jasper.

Karla leaned over, her dark brown eyes gazing directly into Peri's. She woke with a start. The only eyes gazing soulfully at her from the next pillow were Jasper's green orbs.

Dreams of Karla were less frequent now but no less disturbing. The numerals on the clock showed 01:58. Peri doubted she would get back to sleep easily.

"Stay here Jasper. I'm just going to the loo." Great. Now I'm talking to the cat as if expecting him to understand the words. Not long until Dana and Sharon arrive. She needed some adult conversation soon.

†

Rory dried the dishes on automatic pilot. Walking back from Sheepfold Grange, he'd wondered why he found it so hard to bring up the subject he really wanted to talk to Peri about. It should be easier talking to someone he hadn't known forever. Next time he saw her, he would do it. He had to talk to someone for the sake of his own sanity.

"I think it's dry now." Bean's voice reached him from far away.

He looked down at the plate in his hands. "Oh, yeah." Rory added it to the pile on the counter.

"You okay, Rors?"

"Yeah. Just thinking about a storyline."

"Must be a good one. You looked like you'd gone into outer space there. Sure you're not tripping like Adam?"

Rory almost lost his grip on the glass he'd picked up. "How do you know about that?"

"Jeez, I've got a nose, haven't I? He needs to be more careful. Jude's sister asked me to tell him she needs some for her birthday party next week."

"Fuck, no! What did you say?"

"I told her to tell her sister to ask him herself. I'm not getting involved."

"Good for you. I wish..." He put the glass down and picked up the pile of plates to put in the cupboard.

"What?" Bean dried her hands on the dishtowel he'd dropped on the counter. "What do you wish?"

"I wish they wouldn't involve us in this shit. I didn't want to talk to Peri about it, but Dad's worried she'll split."

"I know what you mean. The kittens aren't really ready yet for rehoming. Maybe in another week. But Mum said I had to take Jasper today."

"Jasper?"

"That's what we named the kitten. It suits him."

Rory smiled at his sister. "Good. Hopefully that will help take her mind off the other thing." A small hope, he thought.

The kitten would only provide a short-term distraction from finding out she'd moved next to a cannabis farm.

CHAPTER SEVENTEEN

Dana scooped Jasper up into her arms as soon as she saw him. "Isn't he cute?" She grinned at Peri. "A few more of these and we'll be calling you the crazy cat lady."

"One's enough for now." Peri gave her friend a hug, mindful not to squash the kitten.

Sharon called out from the doorway. "Are you two ready for lunch? I know I am."

Dividing the food they'd brought onto three plates, they sat out on the patio and caught Peri up with their activities of the past two weeks. They'd seen a few films and had dinner out with friends. Peri's only contribution was to show them the greenhouse, the pond, the newly planted seedlings, and her new car.

"You really do need to get out more," Dana said.

"It's okay. I'm keeping busy. I've got two editing jobs coming up as well."

"What about when you're not busy? When the weather turns nasty and you're stuck indoors," Dana countered.

"I've got books to read." She sipped at the crisp, white wine Sharon had poured for them. "And now a cat to talk to."

"Seriously, Peri. What about this walking group you mentioned?"

"I don't know. Maybe in the autumn. I'm just not feeling very sociable at the moment. I thought I might start with the local historical society. They meet once a month."

"Wow. That sounds exciting. I doubt you'll meet many lesbians there."

"I don't want to meet anyone. Not in the way you're implying."

Sharon poured out the last of the bottle, sharing it between the three glasses. "Quite right, Peri. You'll know when you're ready."

"Thank you, Sharon." Peri gave Dana a mock glare. She knew her friend was only trying to help her through the transition from married life to being a singleton again. But she didn't want to even think about meeting someone. At her age, did she really want to go through any of that angst again?

The rain came not long after they finished eating. Taking the plates and glasses inside, Dana disappeared into the kitchen with Jasper. Peri touched Sharon's arm.

"There's something I want to talk to you about." She closed the patio doors and led the way to the sofa.

Sharon joined her. "What is it? You're not having second thoughts about the divorce, are you?" She'd brought documents for Peri to sign. "It looks like Karla's not contesting anything. She's even agreed to give you an equal share from the house sale, when she sells."

"No. It's about my neighbours."

"Oh. Problems in paradise, already?"

"That's just it. They've been so kind to me. They're a lovely family. Even the oldest boy, Adam, has come round. He was wary of me at first. Thought I'd be corrupting his little sister." Peri sighed. "They're not just sheep farmers. They grow marijuana."

"Okay."

"But it's not okay, is it? It's illegal. I can't help wondering if they've been making friends with me to make sure I keep quiet."

"Do they sell it?"

"I guess they do. It's not for family consumption. They do supply it to local people, just for medicinal purposes, so they say. Apparently, it was Martin's father who started growing it back in the sixties. Supplied all his friends."

"And they know that you know about it?"

"Yes."

"How did they react?"

"Very calmly. Just said it was part of the family business. Martin carried on with it when his parents retired. After his mother died, his father moved to Amsterdam. Seems Dad was a sampler of the product."

"How did you find out?"

"I might never have suspected, although all the Rushfords get anxious whenever a helicopter flies down the valley. Hayley gave me some freshly baked brownies, which I liked. I didn't connect the feeling of euphoria I got after eating them until a local cop turned up to inspect my greenhouse. He told me it's well known that there are cannabis farms all through the hills. The locals see themselves as carrying on the coiner tradition."

"Coiner?"

"Yes. They're quite proud of that part of their heritage. David Hartley, king of the coiners, was a local hero." Peri smiled at Sharon's puzzled expression. "Back in the day, it was a way of cheating the revenue. Clipping coins to make new ones was a profitable industry. It might have carried on for longer, had one of the excise men not got too close to exposing the operation. He was shot. David Hartley was eventually captured and hung, although he hadn't done the shooting. He's seen as a martyr, mainly. There are songs and books about him, including a children's book."

"So really, you're up against a long-standing ethos of lawlessness. The natives see nothing wrong with outwitting the authorities."

"Exactly that."

"I think what you have to ask yourself, Peri, is what will you achieve if you turn them in? You'd be breaking up a family. You wouldn't be able to stay here either. The whole community would be affected. I'm guessing it's no secret in the area, if the family has been doing this for generations."

"That's the thing. Quite a few people in the area must know about it. So why haven't they been caught before now? I suspect even that cop who showed up must know. He was at school with Martin and Hayley."

"I suppose the only mitigating circumstance is that what they're supplying is less harmful than the stronger stuff on the streets now that is mixed with synthetics. This homegrown weed will be more like what the hippies were ingesting in the sixties."

"It can still be harmful though. People, especially youngsters, react differently. It's linked now to the increase in teenage depression and suicide."

"It also has some medicinal benefits."

"That's what Martin said. I guess he justifies it by thinking the good outweighs the bad."

Dana came in, trailing a long piece of string. Jasper pounced on the end each time it moved.

"I hope you don't mind, Peri. The little guy claimed he was starving, so I gave him a piece of the leftover chicken."

"Oh no. Now he'll be turning his nose up at the dried stuff and expect a more gourmet diet."

Dana sat next to Sharon and twitched the string again. Jasper jumped, and Dana picked him up and waited for him to settle on her lap. Peri couldn't decide who looked more content, the kitten or her friend.

"What have you done with the pictures you brought from the house? I haven't seen them hanging anywhere."

"I had planned to put one over the fireplace and one on that wall over there. When I looked at them in here, they just felt wrong. Like they don't fit. They're part of my past life. Maybe I should have left them for Karla."

"Well, there seems to be no shortage of artists here. I noticed several galleries in the town. You could get something that's more in keeping with this area."

"Hm. Yes, I could do that."

"How about tomorrow? Sharon hasn't been to lesbo-land yet."

"I wish you wouldn't call it that."

When Peri woke the next morning, she could tell it was going to be another scorcher of a day. After feeding Jasper, she went out to water the plants while it was still cool and before the sun got on them, another of Rory's gardening tips.

It was after ten before her guests were ready to set off on the trip to town. Peri persuaded them to walk in. She left Jasper curled up on the sofa. Whether or not he was listening when she told him to be a good boy, time would tell. He hadn't left any deposits in the house yet, but there was always a first time.

"Why can't we drive? Give your car a run?" Sharon asked.

"Parking anywhere close is a nightmare on the weekend, unless you go in early. We can get the bus back."

The stroll along the canal towpath wasn't too taxing. They stopped every now and again to take photos of ducks and geese and narrow boats.

"I'm going to need a café stop," Sharon exclaimed when they reached the town centre. "I haven't breathed in this much fresh air since our holiday last year in Devon."

Peri led them into one of the coffee shops she hadn't been in yet. Glancing around while Sharon ordered their drinks, she noticed several paintings displayed on the walls. She moved closer to inspect one that drew her eye and saw that it was for sale.

"That's really nice. I can see it looking good over your fireplace." Dana stood behind her.

"Yeah. I think so too. We might not make it to any galleries."

When the server brought their order to the table, Peri asked about the painting.

"Actually, it's textile art. If you look closely you can see the threads. The artist lives locally, and we have more of her work on the wall going upstairs. She offers prints as well, if the originals are out of your price range."

"I would love to support a local artist. Could you put that one on hold for me? I'll give you my details before we leave."

By the time they left the coffee shop, Peri had arranged to buy two canvases and a time to collect them during the week.

"Well, that was easy," Sharon commented as they walked down the street. "How about you show us around, now we don't need to look at more pictures."

"Yes. We could go up to Heptonstall. I haven't been there yet myself, but I gather it's a lovely old village with fantastic views."

"Oh, that sounds good. Is it far?"

"Only about half a mile away." Peri grinned mischievously. "Straight up that hill."

Sharon groaned. "I'll never make it up there."

"Don't fret. There is a bus."

A walk around the hilltop village, taking in the remains of the mediaeval church, Sylvia Plath's grave, the views across the valley and the moorland...and they were ready for a pub lunch. Peri was pleased they'd arrived early enough to get a seat in the garden area. Basking in the sun with her friends, with a cold beer and good food, she experienced a feeling of happiness she wouldn't have thought possible a few days earlier. She knew the hurt from Karla's deceptions would never disappear completely, but she could move on with her life. This move to the country was truly the start of new beginnings. Who was she to judge the illicit activities of her neighbours? She was the incomer who needed to adapt to a different environment.

†

Rory propped himself up on one elbow. Why did life have to be so complicated? It was a perfect summer's day, bright and hot. Going for a dip in the res with his mates was the perfect way to spend it. How long would they be his mates if they knew that the boner stretching his shorts like a tent pole wasn't a reaction to the female flesh on show?

He'd been in love with his best friend since their first day at primary school. There was no way Rory could ever tell him that. Trav would probably kill him. That might be preferable to the torture of seeing him wrapped around his girlfriend every day at school and now at the swimming hole. There was no escape.

"Coming in, Ror?" Trav had untangled himself from Bethany's grip and was standing over him, grinning.

"Nah. You go ahead."

Bethany's friend, Sian, was staring at him. He gave her a weak smile. The choices were narrowing. Stay on the sand with the two girls, who thought he was enmeshed in their feminine charms, or follow Trav into the res and hope the shock of hitting the cold water would quickly douse his erection.

"Oh, look. Is that a heron?" He pointed to the sky. When both girls looked up, he stood and sprinted. His PE teacher would be astounded, as Rory had never shown such a burst of speed in any track trials. Rory hit the water at a run. He didn't have time to gasp at the balls-numbing coldness that gripped his body. The cold achieved the desired effect, and he enjoyed a mad ten minutes of splashing around with Trav.

Rory arrived back home with a few hours to spare before the evening meal. He showered before settling down in his room to work on his novel. He read through the last paragraph he'd written, then deleted it. Nothing was working. His dad had quizzed him after he came back from Peri's the other day, but Rory couldn't give him any reassurance that their neighbour wasn't going to blab.

He'd thought about going back to try again, but there was a strange car in the yard when he'd returned from the reservoir. With a final look at the gaping blank space in front of him, he closed the laptop and decided a walk might help revive the creative juices.

Mum was in the kitchen, a tomato sauce bubbling away in a pan. She looked up from stirring. "All right, love?"

"Yeah. Just going out for a walk."

"You might want a coat. It looks like rain coming."

Rory glanced out the window. Dark clouds were hovering over the hills.

"Okay. I won't be long."

The rain came slanting across the valley before he reached the end of the first field. The anorak he'd grabbed from the coat rack on his way out wasn't adequate for the onslaught, and he arrived back in the house dripping from head to toe. The soaking had sparked an idea for his story. After a quick towel off and change of clothes, the words poured out of his fingers to make patterns on the screen.

PART TWO

CHAPTER EIGHTEEN

Peri fell asleep in her recliner, again. It was only midafternoon. Even though the summer's activities meant she was fitter than she'd ever been ...planting and harvesting her vegetables, hiking with the walking group every Thursday, and enjoying bike rides on nice evenings...she found she needed a nap every now and again.

The winter months would bring new challenges, but she felt ready to take on whatever might come. Sharon didn't foresee any difficulties with the divorce, as Karla wasn't contesting it. Peri knew it was time to start looking forward instead of back. She'd experienced a stark reminder of this a few days earlier, when she remembered it was Karla's birthday. She took out the necklace she'd bought for her so many months ago from its place in her bedside table. Peri couldn't think of anyone she could give it to. Perhaps she should see what a local jeweller would offer.

It was the beginning of October, and the sale of the house had gone through without a hitch. A large amount of money was now sitting in her bank account, so she needed to think about how to invest it. She was reluctant to contact Martin's friend, Phil. Although Peri maintained a friendly face towards the family members, she didn't want to be any more reliant on them. She should talk to Sharon.

She awoke from her nap to see someone staring in at her from the garden. Heart pounding, Peri struggled out of the chair and rubbed her eyes for a clearer look.

The person was smiling, and it only took a moment to see it was a young woman wearing a huge backpack. Peri smiled back, but she wasn't buying anything. Really, she thought she would be safe from door-to-door sellers at the cottage. Might just be a misguided rambler.

She approached the open doorway cautiously. "Hi. Can I help you?"

"Peri Sanderson?"

"Um. Yes."

"Sorry to disturb you like this. I'm Rhiannon. Your niece."

"My niece?"

"Well, one of them anyway."

The accent woke up Peri's sluggish brain cells. "From Canada?"

"Yes."

"Wow. You've come a long way." *Understatement of the year. Wake up, Peri.* "Do come in." She stood aside and waited, while the girl shrugged off her pack before entering.

"Would you like a drink?"

"Sure. A cold beer if you've got one."

Peri fetched a Corona from the fridge and poured herself a glass of water.

"Hope this is okay. Sorry I haven't got a lime or lemon."

"No worries." Rhiannon took the bottle from her and chugged back a good portion of it. She wiped her lips with the back of her hand. "Thanks. I needed that. It's a bit of trek up that hill."

Peri sat back in her recliner again. "I've lost touch with the family. How many siblings do you have?"

"There are four of us. I'm the youngest. I started out doing a gap year, but it's sort of turned into two. I've been working my way across Canada for the past eighteen months, but the main purpose for my trip was to come to England to find our mysterious, unknown aunt."

Peri looked at her niece in the fading light. She could see the resemblance to her brother in the eyes and the mouth. Rhiannon's short-cropped hair showed traces of red, which looked natural. Her mother's side, likely.

"Could I see your passport? Not that I don't believe you are who you say you are, but this is a bit of a shock for me."

"Oh. Of course." The girl dug around in the bumbag she'd discarded after sitting down. "Here you go. I guess, living up here on your own, you can't be too careful. Random walkers turning up."

Peri flipped the document open to the page with the photo and personal details, then looked at the back page. The next of kin contacts included the names of both her brother and mother. She handed it back to Rhiannon.

"They never talked about me?"

"No. It was as if you didn't exist. When I first saw the photos Grandpa had kept, I thought perhaps you'd died."

"I was dead to them. After I came out to my parents, they couldn't emigrate quickly enough. I know that sounds overly dramatic. They were always going to follow Rick to Canada, and the imminent birth of their first grandchild was the main incentive."

When the girl told her about finding the battered envelope her father had kept, hidden behind some books in his den, Peri felt a surge of pain. The totality of her family's rejection still hurt after all these years. That she hadn't even been told her father was dead was another blow, more evidence of how completely she'd been cut out of their lives.

"Grandma told me to burn the envelope. She had only glanced at the photo I'd pulled out and didn't want to see the letters."

"Did you burn them?"

"No. I managed to smuggle the envelope to my room. After I read the letters, I confronted my dad. I asked why we knew nothing about an aunt, his only sister. Was she still alive? He said he neither knew nor cared. End of subject. Mum was more forthcoming. She said you were the black sheep of the family. The last communication was a letter telling them you were marrying your long-term partner. Well, a civil-partnership ceremony anyway. That letter went straight into the fire."

Peri snorted. "I suspected as much. I don't really know why I wrote. I'd only sent one letter before then, congratulating them on the birth of their first child. It was never acknowledged even though I enclosed my email address. Perhaps I was hoping their views on same-sex relationships might have softened over time."

"Not likely to ever happen, I'm afraid. Even though same-sex marriage has been legal in Canada for a long time now. I thought about telling them I'm bi, just for the shock factor. I chickened out."

"How did you find me? Those early letters were the ones I wrote from university."

"I Googled your name, of course. You don't have a digital footprint, but Karla's all over the net. Surprisingly, Mum remembered her name from your letter. Anyway, I soon found out where she worked."

"So much for any privacy online." Peri shook her head. "How did Karla react when you showed up at her office?"

"Not exactly welcoming. Couldn't get rid of me fast enough. She gave me this address and told me to fuck off."

Rhia reached into her backpack and opened one of the inside, zipped pockets. She handed an worn brown envelope to Peri. "Grandpa's letters."

Peri's tears leaked out then. "I can't believe he kept these. I wish I'd known he still cared, in his own way."

"I think he kept a lot to himself. I wish I'd talked to him more before he passed."

"How did he die?"

"Painlessly, it seems. Just went to sleep in his armchair one evening and didn't wake up. He'd not shown any signs of heart problems. Grandma took it hard, even though she mostly moaned about him while he was alive. It took her a year to get around to sorting out his things. It will be three years in November since he died."

Peri put the envelope she'd been clutching tightly onto the table next to her chair. Time to revisit those memories later.

"You must be hungry. How about we go into town for something to eat? I haven't got much food in."

"Yeah, that would be ace."

"Good. The guest room's the door on the right at the top of the stairs. And the bathroom's at the end of the passage."

"Would it be okay to have a shower? I feel a bit grungy."

"Of course. Towels are in the cupboard on the landing." Peri was glad she'd remembered to retrieve extra towels and sheets from the London house before the sale went through. Karla had told her to come and collect whatever else she wanted. Anything that was left would be going into storage.

"Perfect." Rhiannon stood and easily lifted the heavy-looking pack.

"Just come down when you're ready. There's no rush. I need to leave food out for Jasper."

"Oh. Is he a dog or a cat?"

"A cat. And he may be sleeping on your bed. I hope you're not allergic."

"Not a problem. We have cats and dogs at home." Rhiannon turned and trotted up the stairs.

Peri hadn't eaten out in the evening, other than at the Rushford farm, so she made a quick search of restaurants in the area while Rhiannon was showering. There were quite a variety of options in the town...Italian, Thai, Turkish. If they were all booked up, there were several large pubs. She wouldn't bother booking. They could just go in and see what caught their fancy.

What had prompted the youngster to seek her out? Over dinner, she would try to find out. She knew she'd been airbrushed out of existence in her family history. It was one of the things that drew her and Karla together when they first met. Although Karla's family hadn't rejected her outright, they were split. She and her sister had an on-off relationship and generally only met up with their father for Christmas and birthdays. As Peri had recently discovered, even that didn't happen anymore. Once again, she found herself wondering how many years Karla had been deceiving her, using family reunions to cover for another affair.

Rhiannon appeared in the kitchen looking cleaner and wearing a tank top and shorts.

"Will you be warm enough?"

"Sure. That's a very aunt-like thing to say."

"It is, isn't it? Bear with me. I haven't had any practice at being an aunt."

"Time to get started then. Where are we going?"

Peri was glad she had chosen an automatic. The car handled well and was much easier to park than the Range Rover. They'd decided on trying the Italian first. As they walked through the square, Peri marvelled that she felt so at ease. Any fears that she might miss living in London were unfounded. If it hadn't been for Karla's job, they could have moved out to the countryside years ago. Karla wouldn't have lasted. Maybe then their marriage would never have happened.

No point pondering the what-ifs. Peri led the way up the stone steps to the restaurant, opening the door on the sounds of people talking and laughing and the rich aroma of garlic and spices. It was already busy at only six thirty, but they were in luck and were able to have a table, as long as they were finished by eight.

Peri ordered the Merlot. Surrounded by the warm ambience and with the company of the young woman seated opposite, Peri felt there was nowhere else she wanted to be.

Everything happened for a reason. She could never have imagined she would be sitting in a restaurant with her niece, making a connection with the family that had rejected her.

Once they were seated at their table with a glass of wine each and warm bread to nibble, Peri asked the question that was uppermost in her mind. "You've gone to a lot of trouble to find me and travelled all this way. I guess I really want to know why."

"I grew up thinking my parents were fairly open-minded liberals." Rhia paused to spread some butter on her bread. "But when one of my best friends in high school came out as gay, they didn't want me to have anything more to do with him. We had some massive rows about that. I kept seeing him, secretly, of course. So when I found out that I had a lesbian aunt…"

"You wouldn't have known that from reading those letters. I wrote those before I came out to the family."

"I know. Dad's reaction made me suspicious, then Mum revealed that you had married a woman. So, I wanted to meet you."

The waiter brought their starters, and Peri was glad for a distraction. "What do you plan to do next, once the novelty of meeting your long-lost aunt wears off?"

They spent a pleasurable hour discussing various places to visit in the British Isles, then moved on to Europe. Peri hadn't travelled much abroad. Family holidays took place at caravan sites in Devon and Cornwall. When she started working after uni, she couldn't afford anything exotic, only a few weekends away to Paris, Amsterdam, and Berlin. Karla's work took her all over the world, so she hadn't wanted to make any long-haul trips during her holiday times. They did make it to the south of France once, early on in their relationship. Ironic, considering where Karla's infidelities first came to light.

†

Karla sat by the fountain and trailed her fingers through the water. This part of the garden was hidden from the house, and she was happy to have the space to herself. Meeting Syd's parents and older brothers had been daunting enough, but there were other guests. All had titles of some description, all present and future denizens of the House of Lords. And all with the same purpose of drinking as much champagne as they could when they weren't snorting cocaine.

Although she loved being with Syd, the glamour of associating with the rich and famous was waning. She'd managed to limit herself to one glass of champagne and avoided inhaling any white powder. Syd had made her try coke when they were in Monaco. Karla didn't like the experience of not feeling in control, other than when they were having mind-blowing sex. That was different, giving her lover access to all parts of her body.

When they drove up the long drive to the manor, Karla was reminded of their civil partnership. The ceremony took place on a beautiful day like this in a similar venue. Peri had planned everything, as usual, taking care of all the details. All Karla had to do was wear the outfit, repeat the vows, and mingle with the guests afterwards. Not that there had been many. No one from Peri's family came, and only two from her own. Her brother, Mateo, happened to be visiting friends in London. Valeria came without her husband. Karla hadn't

145

expected either of her parents to attend, but it hurt all the same when they both gave excuses.

Peri had been so excited about the whole thing. Karla played her part, not wanting to disappoint her. She twisted the ring on her finger. They'd converted the civil partnership to a marriage several years later. She couldn't bring herself to remove the ring, even though she knew there was no going back.

What happened to make her abandon the vows she made on that day? It wasn't Peri's fault that Karla couldn't control her desire for a varied sex life. That's how she reconciled her behaviour to herself. Sometimes she liked to be the dominant partner, but with Syd she enjoyed being dominated. Peri's gentle, tender approach to lovemaking, although lovely, couldn't satisfy Karla's more primal urges.

Like everyone she'd ever read about in this situation, the only thing that mattered was not getting caught. She should have known it would happen eventually. She couldn't even deny anything, with all the evidence Peri had obtained.

Peri deserved better. She had always been Karla's safety net. Once they were finally divorced, that would be gone forever. Syd certainly wasn't the marrying kind.

The sound of footsteps on the path disturbed her reverie. They stopped before reaching the open space around the fountain. The first voice she heard was Damian's, the eldest brother she'd met on arrival.

"Well chosen, Syd. She's perfect."

Karla didn't hear Syd's response, as their footsteps receded down another path. Both brothers had given her the once over when she was introduced, but she was used to appreciative male gazes. These had held something different.

Perhaps they thought Syd had picked up some tart off the streets. Nice to know they approved of her.

A large gilt-framed painting of their ancestor, Rufus Devereaux, dominated the entrance hall. He had been awarded the manor and lands for services rendered in William the Conqueror's successful invasion. Karla did wonder how they knew what he looked like. They didn't have phones for taking selfies in 1066. The so-called portrait was probably painted sometime in the 1700s when displaying such ostentatious imagery was popular amongst the landed gentry.

She was quizzed on her own family background during the pre-dinner drinks. They soon lost interest on learning that her father was a retired banker and her mother ran a bar in Málaga. Karla couldn't offer much information on the Spanish connection. The last time she'd spent any time there was during a school holiday when she was fifteen. She hadn't wanted to go, as she'd been invited to spend a few weeks at a friend's family farm in Somerset. Not that she was interested in horses, but she had a massive crush on Heather. Just the thought of what could happen in a hayloft kept her awake at nights. She'd read *Lady Chatterley's Lover* and fancied playing the role of the amorous gamekeeper.

For all that, it was Peri who had brought her out of the closet, almost ten years later. So much suppressed desire that exploded once Peri showed her the way.

"Hey, babe. I've been looking all over for you."

Karla opened her eyes at the sound of Syd's voice.

"Have you been through the maze yet?

"No."

"Come on." Syd grasped her hand and pulled her up.

Karla had no idea how many turns they made before reaching the space in the centre. Syd stripping off and commanding her to do the same immediately distracted her. "Relax, babe. No one can see us in here." Syd's hands were already roaming across her breasts. Karla felt the now familiar response in her abdomen. By the time Syd's fingers were pushing into her vagina, she was wet enough to receive the three digits willingly.

Her cries of ecstasy startled a number of birds nesting in the maze's hedge. Maybe they couldn't be seen from the house, but anyone wandering through the grounds could have heard her. Finally spent and gazing up at the circle of sky, Karla knew she would never find her way out without Syd's guidance.

CHAPTER NINETEEN

Rhia sat on the low stone wall, gazing out over the field at sheep grazing in the distance. Finding the aunt no one ever talked about had been a bittersweet experience.

Peri was totally cool. Rhia loved spending time with her aunt but sensed that her presence only brought back memories of the family's rejection. Rhia thought that showing her some photos of their life in Canada might help. Peri had glanced through them, politely smiling and nodding, as Rhia named her siblings and the various animals that lived on the farm. She didn't seem interested in knowing anything more than what was evident on the surface, a seemingly happy, smiling group of people she had no connection with.

Although Peri busied herself with her work, the garden and other activities, there was still the underlying sadness of going through a divorce. None of Rhia's relationships had lasted long enough for her to really know how this would feel. She sensed the older woman's pain whenever they were out in the town. They'd see couples holding hands and sharing laughter at something one of them said, especially if it were two women. Rhia liked to think that her visit had helped Peri, at least in some small way.

Getting to know the Rushford family had added another layer of enjoyment to her travels in this part of England. Adam had even shown her how to build a stone wall. Rhia knew she needed to move on though. The travel bug was nipping at her heels again.

Time to get a few things sorted. Rhia stepped down off the wall and walked back to the cottage. She didn't think Peri would mind if she borrowed her bike to go into town and pick up some necessities.

†

Peri had hoped her niece would stay at least until the start of the New Year, but Rhia was determined to set off. Peri enjoyed her company and time passed quickly. Rhia tried to give her an insight into the other members of her distant family. Peri couldn't work up any enthusiasm over people she wasn't likely to meet. Rhia had even offered to share a Skype session with the family, but Peri hadn't felt ready to face her mother and brother.

Rhia returned from her shopping expedition in time for lunch. They had just settled down with beer and sandwiches, when a helicopter buzzed overhead. The craft hovered a while, near the entrance to the Rushford farm, before moving off down the valley.

Not long after she arrived, Peri had told Rhia about the presence of helicopters in the area and Martin's reaction earlier in the summer, when he'd made a hasty phone call. Rhia's response wasn't what she expected.

"Yeah, I guess he would be worried. I noticed the smell right away. Adam usually reeks of it. Although he tries to cover it up by smoking regular cigs."

"What smell?"

"Weed. Marijuana. You're such an innocent, for someone who's lived in a city. You do know that's why the cops call this area happy valley. Like the TV series. That's where they got the name. There are cannabis farms all over these hills. Martin would have called Hayley to switch off the generator, in case the helicopter got close enough to register the heat."

Peri hadn't given much thought to exactly where they grew the crop. "Have you seen it, you know, where they grow it?"

"Yes. It's well hidden, in a copse of trees. It just looks like a derelict shepherd's hut, so it's not very big. Even if the cops did find it, the Rushfords could say they grow it for their own use."

No surprise that Rhiannon knew so much about what went on at the farm in the short time since she'd turned up. She had been helping with odd jobs, and Adam had showed her how to build a dry stone wall. Rhia was full of enthusiasm for creating a feature at the end of the vegetable patch. That would have to wait until she returned from her European adventure. If she returned.

Peri sensed a wanderlust in the girl that might never be fully satisfied. "Did you get everything you need?"

"Yes. Just have to repack the rucksack, and I'm good to go."

"What time do you need to be at the train station tomorrow?"

Rhia hesitated. "Getting the eight o'clock from Halifax. But you don't need to worry. Adam's giving me a lift."

"Okay. You will keep in touch, won't you?" Peri hoped she didn't sound too much like an anxious parent.

†

Peri hugged herself against the morning chill, as she waved to the retreating farm truck. Neither of the occupants waved back. She would miss Rhia's presence. The last few weeks with her niece had shown how much she missed having someone else around. But she did have Jasper to talk to.

She busied herself clearing up their breakfast dishes and changing the sheets on the guest room bed. It was a good drying day. When she was hanging the clean linen out on the line, she heard the farm vehicle coming back up the track. A grating gear change made her wonder if Adam had indulged in a smoke on the way back from the station. She hoped he would have enough sense not to do it in his dad's truck. The smell would linger for days.

Rhia would be on the train now, heading for London and the start of her continental tour. Although she knew the girl was a seasoned single traveller, Peri couldn't help worrying about her safety.

†

A loud banging on the patio doors roused Peri from her late afternoon nap. She opened her eyes and stumbled to her

Country Living

feet. Martin barged into the living room, followed closely by Hayley.

"Did you know about this?" He thrust a mobile phone in her face.

"About what?"

"Adam's gone with your Rhia. Just got this text message."

"What? He was only taking her to the station. I heard your truck come back this morning."

"Well, someone else must have driven it."

Hayley subsided onto the sofa. "I don't understand. He was saving up to buy his own vehicle. It's all he's ever talked about spending money on since he was twelve."

"I'm sorry. I didn't know he was planning to go with her. She only gave me a vague idea of places she wanted to visit. No mention of anyone else being with her."

"You must have some idea? Where would they be now?"

Peri looked at her watch. "She did tell me Paris was the first stop. I know she'd booked to go on the Eurostar this afternoon. Have you tried calling Adam?"

"Yes, of course. He must have switched his phone off after sending the message."

"I'll try Rhia." Peri picked up her phone and found Rhia's name in her contacts. The call went to voicemail. She left a message, keeping her voice level. "Hope the journey's gone well. Call me when you can." Peri looked at the two anxious faces. "They may have switched off their phones to save on roaming charges."

Hayley dropped her head into her hands. "He's never shown any interest in going anywhere. The farm...that's all he wanted to do. The only time he's been out of the country

153

was when he and his mates went to Ibiza for a week to celebrate the end of their schooldays."

"Rhia travelled across Canada on her own. I'm sure she can handle most situations. Starting in France is good as well. She speaks French."

"I didn't think they were that close." Martin spoke quietly, anger still simmering beneath the surface of his words. "I thought she was like you."

"Um. Well, sort of. She told me she's more on the bi or pan spectrum." Seeing their puzzled looks Peri added, "What we used to call AC/DC."

"Why did she have to pick on our Adam? He's such an innocent. Never had a steady girlfriend." Hayley sniffed into the tissue she'd pulled out of her pocket.

Mothers and sons. Peri didn't think Adam had lived as a celibate monk through his teenage years. Most likely just hadn't brought any of his conquests home.

†

The Rushfords were finally convinced Peri knew as little as they did about Adam's abrupt departure. After they left, she tried Rhia's phone again. Still going to voicemail. She typed out a text with the same wording as the message she'd left earlier. Sooner rather than later, the girl would switch back on to post photos, if nothing else.

Rory stopped by after school. The late afternoon sun warmed the patio, and they sat outside with a glass of orange juice each. Peri was used to Rory's silences. He would speak when he was ready. Each time his visit ended, she felt he'd left something unsaid.

Today was different somehow, then it dawned on her. "You drove the pickup back this morning, didn't you?"

"Yeah, I guess you heard." He looked sheepish. "I did okay on the road, but forgot about changing into low gear on this last bit up the hill."

"That was dangerous. They shouldn't have asked you to do that."

"I wasn't going to. Adam threatened to tell Mum and Dad and my mates about me."

The elephant in the room had grown every time Rory visited her. He seemed ready to open up now, so she kept quiet and waited.

"When did you know that you were gay?" he asked, staring into his glass.

"I suppose it was always there. I just didn't have a name for it until high school."

"When did you come out?"

"While I was at uni."

"How did your parents react?"

"Total rejection. They moved to Canada, and we lost contact."

"Shit." He looked ready to cry.

Peri put a hand on his arm. "Your parents aren't like that. Mine were very religious. This is a different time and place as well. My friend from London calls this town lesbo heaven. I know there's a Pride festival every year now."

"I know. But it doesn't mean everyone's so accepting. Especially people you've known all your life. What if they hate me for it?"

"This probably sounds trite, but really, it's their problem, not yours. You need to be able to be true to yourself. To express who you are. If they don't like that, then they're not true friends. Your parents seemed to accept me when I first arrived. Have they ever made homophobic comments?"

"No. Adam does though. And they've never told him off about it. So maybe they agree with him."

"Your brother has a very narrow world view. This trip with Rhia may be a good thing and open his eyes to different experiences."

"Maybe." He didn't look convinced.

"Have you read any books by gay authors?"

"No. Not something they stock in the school library."

"Wait here." Peri went into the house and quickly found Armistead Maupin's *Tales of the City* and the latest Patrick Gale novel.

Rory looked them over. "I've heard of these." He tapped the cover of the large, three-volume hardback of *Tales of the City*. "Wasn't there a TV series?"

"Yes. You might be able to get some clips of the original series on YouTube. I suppose they'll look rather dated to you, seventies and eighties clothes and hairstyles, but the stories are good."

He smiled, and this time the expression did reach his eyes. "Thank you."

"You're welcome. Try not to worry. You never know, talking to your parents might help. Maybe start by telling your mum. Men sometimes find it harder to accept. Sometimes they react badly, because they're concerned you'll get hurt. They want you to have what they think of as a normal life."

"Yeah, I suppose. I better get going. Thanks for everything." Rory gathered the books into his rucksack. He stepped easily over the boundary wall and waved as he set off up the field to the farm.

CHAPTER TWENTY

A motorhome painted with a large rainbow on the side was parked by the gate. Peri wasn't expecting anyone. Rhiannon had only been gone a week and was somewhere in Europe, unless she'd run out of money already.

Peri leant the bike against the wall by the front door, took the parcel she'd collected out of the pannier and hurried into the kitchen.

"Rhia?"

No answer. The living room was empty too, but there was a stranger standing in the garden by the edge of the pond. Laying the parcel on a table, Peri opened the door and stepped out onto the patio.

"Hello."

The woman turned, a smile on her face. She had an abundance of laugh lines around the eyes and mouth.

Peri had no problem placing her then, the resemblance to Hayley was remarkable. The hair was shorter, cut in a stylish layered bob. The familiar features weren't the only thing that made Peri think she'd seen her before, somewhere.

"Hi, I didn't mean to intrude. Just curious to see what's been done to this place since my last visit."

"Oh, you must be Nan. I'm Peri."

"Nan I don't mind from the family. In the outside world, I'm known as Raven."

The name and the face clicked. "Raven Skybird. I saw you at Edinburgh some years ago."

"Did you enjoy the performance? If it was a long time ago, it was probably pretty dire. I think I've improved over the years."

"It was…memorable."

Raven threw back her head and laughed. When she recovered, she smiled at Peri. "Memorable. Is that your version of utter crap?"

"Well…um…it wasn't really my thing. Anyway, would you like to see inside?" Peri could feel her cheeks flaming.

"Sure, thanks."

After the tour, they sat on the patio to enjoy some red wine in the last of the afternoon sunshine. It was just warm enough for sitting out with their coats on. Jasper occupied his favourite spot by the pond. Peri had noticed that the birds stayed away when the cat was in residence.

Raven took a sip from her glass. "This is pretty nice. I'm sure I don't warrant being served your best vintage."

"My ex had good taste. I'm not so particular, but it seems a shame to keep it for a special occasion that might not happen any time soon."

"Where's your ex now?"

"Somewhere in London. She sold our house last month, and I've no idea where she's living now."

"Were you together a long time?"

"Twenty years."

"Wow, that's tough. I'm sorry."

"She was a lying, cheating, manipulative bitch. But I miss her." Tears pricked her eyes. This was the first time she'd said those words out loud, admitting her innermost feelings to a stranger.

Raven laid a hand on her arm. "Hey, it's okay. I've always thought the time-heals-all adage is overrated."

"It's only been five months. The divorce hasn't gone through yet. It shouldn't be much longer before it's officially ended."

"That's still quick for a divorce."

"Well, with all the evidence stacked up against her, she can't fight it."

They sat in silence for a few minutes, listening to the birds and the occasional soft bleating of the sheep in the nearest field.

"What brings you here now? I was told you don't visit very often." Peri set her empty glass on the table. Her visitor frowned, gazing into the distance.

"Hayley called. They're worried about Adam going off with your niece. And about you."

"Me?"

"Yes. Now you know about the pot business, they think you might go to the cops."

"I've known about it for some time. If I were going to spill the beans, I'd have done it already."

"That's what I told them, even without knowing you."

"I like living here. I like the family. If I'm honest, I actually enjoyed the brownies Hayley gave me. I have to drink quite a lot of wine to get the same euphoric effect."

Raven grinned. "Wonderful. That's one less thing for her to worry about then."

"I don't know why they're so concerned about Adam. Rhia will take care of him to start with, and he'll learn how to handle himself in different situations."

"Again, that's what I told those two. I was concerned that the boy never went through a rebellious stage earlier. He's obviously just a late starter. I've no doubt he'll get this out of his system and come back to the farm. If he doesn't, well, it's not the end of the world."

"I suppose it would seem like that to Martin. I'm sure he expects Adam to take over from him, eventually. Rory's not interested, and I don't know about Bean."

"You never know. She might surprise them."

Peri refilled their glasses, and the conversation turned to Raven's life on the road...the pros and cons of living in a van for part of the year. She generally stayed at the farm during the coldest part of the winter. That used to be November and December but shifts in the climate meant it was now January and February. She did like to spend Christmas with the family.

By the time Raven left, Peri felt she'd made a friend and was looking forward to having someone her own age nearby.

†

160

Raven parked by the barn and met her daughter coming out the front door. After a quick hug, she followed Hayley into the kitchen.

"Good timing. I've just taken this batch out." She pointed to the tray of brownies cooling on a rack on the counter.

"They smell good. But I'll have to sample them later. I've just had a few glasses of wine with your neighbour at Sheepfold."

"Peri?"

"Yes."

"I'm not sure you should have done that. She already thinks we send the kids there to spy on her."

"As it happens, we had a very nice conversation. You don't need to worry about your production line." Raven pointed to the brownies. "She confessed to actually liking them. Gave her quite the buzz."

"Oh, well that's good then. Tea, coffee?"

"Just water for now, love. That wine was quite strong." Raven sat down at the table. Hayley poured water for both of them and they spent the next ten minutes catching up. Raven relaxed into the familiar farmhouse smells overlaid with the freshly baked hash brownies. In a lull in their conversation, Hayley got up to check on the next batch in the oven. Raven's mind wandered back to meeting the woman now living at Sheepfold Grange. From Hayley's near hysterical phone call a few days earlier, Raven had expected to meet an old crone. Instead, she'd been beguiled by the incomer. The lines around her eyes crinkled when she smiled. There was no doubt she had a sense of humour, but there was the underlying sadness when the subject of her ex came up.

"How long can you stay?"

Hayley's question brought her back to the kitchen.

"I'm not sure. A few weeks, at least. It may depend on the weather. I will be back for Christmas." She reached across the table and patted her daughter's arm. "I'm sure Adam will be back by then, too."

"I don't know. Maybe he's so enamoured of this girl that he'll follow her anywhere. I just didn't see it coming." Tears were starting to run down her cheeks.

Raven leant forward and grasped both Hayley's hands in her own. "Oh, sweetheart. He'll be back. He's a farm boy at heart. Young love can be a treacherous thing. It may not have even survived the train journey through the tunnel." She released Hayley's hands to give her the chance to wipe away her tears with a dishtowel. "Now, tell me how Rory and Bean are doing."

†

The next week passed quickly for Peri. Raven invited her to an open mic at the local wine bar. Although she had seen it advertised, Peri hadn't been to one before. They had a lot of fun, and Raven did a turn as well, eliciting much laughter and applause from the audience.

The following day Raven suggested a walk to one of the local landmarks, Gibson Mill. The path beside Hebden Water wasn't too arduous, although a bit muddy in places. Raven shared her knowledge of the area's history.

"How do you know so much?" Peri asked.

"I worked part-time in the tourist office for a bit. Have you been up to Stoodley Pike yet?"

"No. I've been meaning to go." Peri really had meant to make the trek up to the monument that was visible on top of

162

the hill between Hebden Bridge and Todmorden. Rhia had been and told her it was worth the climb.

"You do wonder, though, don't you? Why are these memorials always so phallic in design?"

Peri laughed. "Well, it's men who design and erect them."

"Erect being the operative word."

"Did you know there are numerous drawings of pricks on Hadrian's Wall? The Roman soldiers put them there as it was a symbol of good luck, and they were a superstitious bunch."

"Carried on to this day by schoolboys everywhere, so one of my teacher friends told me. She dreaded handling the boys' exercise books for marking, knowing where they'd been touching themselves in class."

"Ugh. Too much information."

They shared a bottle of beer and sat at one of the outside tables, listening to the sounds of the river and birds calling to each other from the tops of the trees.

"So, what is your real name?" Peri felt it was okay to ask, now that she'd spent time with the woman.

"Raven Skybird is my real name, my two given names anyway. Surname Horsfield. That is what is on my birth certificate. My parents were the original hippies, although they started out as beatniks in the fifties."

"Wasn't that a bit awkward at school?'

"Not really. By the time I started, more hippies had moved into the area. Ordinary Janes and Johns were few and far between. My best friends through primary school were Chico and Lovelace. My name seemed almost normal."

"Poor Lovelace."

"Yeah. She changed her name to Laura before we started high school."

Peri sipped her beer and was thankful Raven didn't ask about her own name. She wasn't ready to admit to being a Pearl quite yet. So far, Bean had kept her secret.

Raven's next question caught her off guard.

"What would your online profile say?

"What?"

"You know…if you registered with a dating app."

"Not you too. My niece tried to talk me into doing that."

"Well, hypothetically speaking, how would you describe the type of person you're looking for?

"I'm not looking for anyone."

"Come on. Humour me."

"Okay." Peri drained her glass and wondered if they should get another one. That half had gone down too quickly, particularly if they were going to pursue this topic. "A good sense of humour, obviously."

"That's too vague. Senses of humour can differ enormously. What is the first thing you notice about a woman…that attracts you?"

Peri looked at her. Was she fishing for compliments? Was this a flirting technique? "Um. The eyes, I guess. And mouth."

"Not a breasts or booty person then?" Raven's eyes sparkled mischievously.

"Booty?"

"Yes, you know. A generous curve of the buttocks highlighted in tight jeans, or better still, lycra."

Peri glanced around the seating area. The nearest couple was two tables away and deep in a conversation of their own. "Do people put that kind of thing on dating sites?"

"I don't know, but you would want to know some important things before setting up a meeting. Like how out of date their profile pic is. If it's even them and not someone else better looking."

"Sounds like it would be a minefield. Although it has worked out for one couple I know." Peri remembered how worried she'd been when Dana told her she'd hooked up with someone she met online. Seeing her and Sharon together for the first time had allayed those fears, and now she couldn't imagine either of them being with anyone else. "Another?" Peri waved the bottle. "This Saltaire Blonde's pretty nice."

"No. Otherwise I'll want to pee before we make it back to town."

They set off along the path beside the river. Walking behind Raven in some places where the path narrowed, Peri found herself watching the movement of Raven's firm butt cheeks in her form-fitting jeans. She had to admit to a burgeoning attraction. Maybe she was a "booty" person after all.

†

A visit from either Bean or Rory after school was a regular occurrence. Peri didn't mind. They were both good company. Bean, particularly, liked to play with Jasper.

Peri was relaxing on the patio after another long hike with Raven. They'd taken the trail over Blackstone Edge. The good weather wasn't going to last, so she wanted to make the most of every day of sunshine.

Bean appeared around the corner of the cottage.

"No Radar today?" Peri looked up from her book.

"No, he's out with Dad." She sounded down.

"What's up? Bad day at school?"

"No." Bean plopped into the other chair with a heavy sigh. "I've started bleeding."

Peri sat up. "Bleeding. Where?"

Bean pointed to her crotch.

"Oh. You mean you've started having periods."

"Yes." The tears started. "Mum says it happens every month for the rest of my life. Is that true?"

"Well, not quite. It's generally a long time though." Peri didn't want to depress the girl any further by voicing the phrase "early start, late finish."

"And she says I have to use pads, not tampons." Bean's anguished gaze caught Peri's. "They smell."

Memories of her schooldays surfaced. Peri remembered the dread of finding red spots on the sheets or when she went to the bathroom. She'd hated the big, bulky pads and suffered through several years before a friend introduced her to tampons and showed her how to insert one.

"Is the bleeding heavy? How often do you have to change the pad?"

"Twice in the morning, then again at dinner time."

The local reference to the midday meal had confused Peri when she first moved to the cottage and heard people talking about dinner when they meant lunch.

"Then I had to change it again after school. I almost missed the bus."

Jasper strolled over to the patio. He sniffed at Bean's ankles, then jumped up onto Peri's lap.

"See, even he can't stand the smell."

Peri thought she was probably overstepping the mark by offering advice, but Hayley was already upset with her over Adam's disappearance. If she was going to be accused of corrupting the Rushford children, she might as well go for the full set.

She stroked Jasper's head. "Look. I don't have any tampons in the house." She'd got off lightly, according to Dana. Her periods just stopped one day, five years ago. No agonising years of hot flushes and extreme mood swings. "I'll pick some up in town tomorrow."

A smile broke out on Bean's face. "You would do that for me?"

"Of course. But don't tell your mum."

"No, I won't. Thank you so much."

"Not a problem. Now you'd better get off home before Hayley thinks I've kidnapped you."

After Bean left, Peri made a note in her phone and set the reminder to buy the necessary item. She didn't want to let the girl down.

Jasper wasn't pleased at being disturbed when she got up to fetch herself a glass of wine. Peri felt in need of a drink after discussing periods with a distressed eleven-year-old. She just hoped she was doing the right thing, encouraging Bean to go against her mother's instructions.

She'd only taken one sip of the wine, when Rory appeared. Peri smiled at him, as he hopped over the garden wall.

"Must be my lucky day. Bean just left."

"Oh, sorry. You don't mind, do you?"

"No, of course not. Would you like something to drink? Other than wine, that is."

"Water's fine. Don't get up. I can fetch it." His bag landed beside the other chair with a heavy clunk.

When he came back, they sat quietly looking over the garden. Jasper had resumed his watching brief by the pond.

"Um. I was wondering if you would mind…" he hesitated, his hand hovering over his bag. "Would you like to read my manuscript? I printed it out. I know it's probably got a lot wrong with it…" His words ran together, and he blushed to the roots of his hair.

Peri took pity on him, knowing only too well from her dealings with other novice writers, how much it had cost him to pluck up the courage to ask the question.

"Yes, I'd love to. I feel honoured that you're offering to let me read your work."

"You might not like it. It's probably not a genre you read."

"My reading is fairly eclectic. I do enjoy a break from lesbian romances."

His whole body relaxed, and he pulled the bundle of pages out of his bag.

Peri looked at the title page. *Burning Time.* "Hm. Interesting title."

"It's from a poem by…"

"Delmore Schwartz."

"You know it?"

"Yes. If I remember rightly, the poem's called 'Calmly We Walk Through This April's Day.'"

"That's the one. I've never met anyone who's even heard of Schwartz."

"I used to read a lot of poetry when I was younger."

They discussed a number of their favourite poets and poems. Peri was impressed by how widely the boy had read. He'd obviously outgrown the range of books available not just in the school library but the one in town as well. She lent him one of her more recently purchased books, which she was sure the local library wouldn't have on their shelves.

Rory's eyes widened when he read the comments on the back cover of *Evolution* by Eileen Myles. He tucked the book away in his bag without saying a word.

CHAPTER TWENTY-ONE

Their last morning in Thailand. They were leaving for the airport shortly, and Syd had gone down to reception to print off their boarding passes. They were too drunk the night before for anything more than a half-hearted attempt at lovemaking before they passed out.

Karla hefted her case onto the bed to put a magazine in the outside pocket. It met some resistance. She was sure she hadn't put anything in there. Her phone charger was in her rucksack. Reaching in, she pulled out a fist-sized baggie filled with a white powder.

"Bloody hell!"

She unzipped her case and took out the top layer of her clothing. That bulging lump hadn't been there when she'd packed her clothes earlier. When had Syd put it there? While she was in the shower?

How long had Syd been gone? She could arrive back any minute. Not a moment to lose. Karla unzipped Syd's case and placed the large packet underneath one of the carefully folded shirts. She zipped the case closed again and stood it back where it had been. She tucked the smaller baggie of powder into the outside pocket.

With trembling hands, she re-zipped her own case and set it next to Syd's. She went into the bathroom to wash her hands. Leaning against the sink, she took several deep breaths. What did Syd have planned for her? Was she just meant to be the stooge?

Syd's familiarity with the city meant she had been there before, likely more than once. If the authorities suspected Syd was a drug smuggler, she could be stopped at the airport. Karla might get her bags through undetected, or she might not. Well, she didn't fancy twenty-five years in a Thai prison. That wasn't the worst she could expect either. They still had the death penalty for drug offences.

With Syd's family background, she had more chance of getting released. Karla would have no chance. She gazed at her face in the mirror, willing herself not to cry. The hardest part would be acting as if nothing was wrong until they got through airport security. If they got through.

A buzzing noise caught her attention. Syd's phone sat on the vanity, face up. The message was from her brother. Karla opened it to read.

Can't meet at airport. Will pick up merch at your place tomoz, 5ish.

Breathing heavily, she leaned back against the sink.

Well chosen, Syd. She's perfect.

The overheard conversation from the family party gained new meaning. Perfect choice, not as a lover, but as a mule. Had none of their time together meant anything to Syd? She picked up the phone, switched if off and stuffed it in her pocket.

Karla checked her face again to make sure her expression wasn't going to give anything away. The door to the suite opened as she emerged from the bathroom, and Syd waved her passport in the air.

"I couldn't book us two seats together, but I did get you a window one."

Karla took the passport from her and glanced at the boarding pass tucked inside. "Thank you. That's very sweet. Where are you sitting then?"

"A few rows back on the aisle. Not a problem. I'm sure I'll sleep most of the way." Syd patted Karla's backside. "You've worn me out."

"I'm sure that's not possible." Karla forced a smile. She didn't miss Syd's quick glance at the cases. They were back where they had been when Syd left, Karla was sure of that.

"Okay. Last pit stop, then we'll head out."

Karla released an inaudible sigh of relief, as Syd went into the bathroom. Zipping her passport into the inside pocket of her backpack, she took the opportunity to do a quick search for any more surprise packages.

"Got everything?"

"Yes. Just checking I put my charger in here."

Syd held her hand in the back of the taxi. "Have you enjoyed Thailand?"

"Yes. It's beautiful here. I can see why you love it."

"We'll do it again, I'm sure." Syd squeezed her hand.

Karla swallowed and kept her gaze on the passing scenery.

Her heart was pounding, as they waited in the long line to go through security. She turned around to say something to Syd and found herself looking at a stranger. A family of four was now between them. She caught Syd's eyes, but she just smiled and shrugged. Syd silently mouthed, *See you on the other side.*

They were separated into different lanes. Maintaining her game face as she went through the security process wasn't easy. When she'd collected her belongings from the conveyer, Karla moved away to a seat against the wall and took a few deep breaths. So far, so good. She put her watch back on. Syd was in line behind the family, waiting for her case to emerge from the scanner. Karla saw the belt stop moving. Two uniformed men arrived with a dog.

Not waiting for Syd to realise what was happening, Karla hurried out of view. Once on the concourse, she considered her next step. When would Syd be allowed to make a phone call? Karla was sure there would be someone waiting to meet her on arrival in London. A change of clothes might help. What could she do about her appearance without bringing attention to herself?

She had wondered why Syd had insisted they buy their fare from London separately. As with this trip, she'd claimed there hadn't been a seat next to Karla's when she booked. Karla was thankful now. If questioned by the police, she could distance herself from any connection.

Dodging into the first toilets she saw, Karla closed the door of a cubicle and took a few deep breaths. First step was removing the SIM card from Syd's phone, which she'd tucked away in her pocket. She then took off the rainbow strap from her suitcase and wrapped both it and the phone in separate wads of toilet paper.

After depositing both items in the bin near the sinks, she washed her hands and checked her appearance in the mirror. First thing she would do on arriving in London would be to find a hairdresser. She located a scrunchie from her backpack and pulled all her hair back from her face into a ponytail.

The large-brimmed sunhat purchased from a kiosk added to her camouflage. She bought a large latte and settled down to wait. Her first-class ticket would have given her access to an executive lounge, but she didn't want to make it easy for anyone to track her down. Karla reached into her bag and checked for messages before switching off. Another task to add to her growing list. A new phone.

Karla breathed a hearty sigh of relief, as she sank back into the taxi's seat. No one had been waiting for her when she emerged from the "nothing to declare" channel.

She opened the door to her flat cautiously. She'd only moved in the week before leaving for Thailand. Boxes everywhere. She'd decided to rent for a while but was pleased when Aldo offered her the use of this place he kept for visiting interns. Nothing fancy, but it met her immediate needs and was handy for the office. Another plus point, as she hadn't bought another vehicle to replace the Range Rover yet.

Leaving the suitcase by the door, she headed for the bathroom. A long hot shower was what she wanted after the seemingly endless journey. If only she could wash away the stress. She hadn't managed much sleep on the plane, although she had numbed some of her worries with the plentiful supply of alcohol. Karla knew from experience that she would have to drink a ton of water to rehydrate.

She was too wired to try sleeping. *Might as well unpack.* Another surprise package caught her eye. She gingerly picked up the brown envelope, hoping it wasn't another cache of white powder. A frisson of fear shot through her abdomen. What if she had been stopped with this? It was almost a relief to find the envelope contained only money. Although, it could have led to some awkward questioning if it had been found in Bangkok.

This was a lot of money, in dollars. Sleep was definitely out of the question now. Time to make some necessary changes.

After the shower and a change of clothes, she left the flat. Her first stop was a currency exchange near Charing Cross, where she could blend in with the tourists. With a good wad of sterling notes in her pocket, she found the nearest phone shop and purchased a cheap model. She'd upgrade later, when she could feel safer. Next stop was a hairdresser. The last time she'd had short hair was when she was ten. She opted for a completely new look. After some discussion, the stylist recommended a buzz cut on one side and a floppy fringe on the other. Karla decided against dyeing her hair.

The Starbucks on Tottenham Court Road offered a quiet place to collect herself. She opened her new phone and tapped in Aldo's personal number. He answered on the third ring.

"If you're selling something, bugger off."

"It's me. Karla."

"Hey, you're back. I didn't recognise this number."

"Yeah, it's a long story, and I need your advice. Can we meet outside the office?"

"Sure. Give me half an hour. Where are you?"

She told him and settled down to wait, hoping the triple shot espresso would keep her awake.

Her eyelids were drooping when his voice startled her.

"I almost didn't recognise you. That's quite a change. What's with the funky style?" Aldo placed two large Americanos on the table.

Karla opened her eyes and waited for him to sit. "Part of my disguise. I may have to emigrate to Patagonia."

"Sounds a bit drastic. What's happened? I thought you were on holiday with your dream woman?"

"The dream that turned into a nightmare." She gave him an abbreviated version of events leading up to her departure from Bangkok.

"Hm." He took a sip of his coffee. "So you were meant to be the mule. And if you were picked up, she would have just walked away."

"Yeah." Karla told him about the separate bookings.

"You think her family will come after you? Is that what you're worried about?"

"I don't know, but I'm not taking any chances."

"How big was the package?"

"I'd say about a kilo. Like a big bag of sugar."

"Mega street value then. Big bucks lost."

Karla nodded. She didn't tell him about the cash she'd found in her case.

"So, what are you going to do? I need you back at work."

"If you can set me up with an alias, I can work remotely. I was thinking of going up north."

He held up his hand. "Don't tell me. The less I know, the better. In case I get a visit from the brothers."

They arranged to meet at King's Cross station the next day. Karla left the coffee shop first and wandered down the street, dodging the phone zombies. Although Syd wouldn't know the address of the company flat, her brothers could track her to the office. The drugs weren't recoverable, but they would surely want the money back.

CHAPTER TWENTY-TWO

Dana had an hour to kill before she could return to collect her iPad. The techie person in the shop didn't think it would take long to find out why the 'home' button wasn't working. She decided the best way to use the time was to sit in Starbucks with a tall latte and write out some character notes for the new novel that had been swirling around in her mind. She missed Peri.

The pastries looked divine. As she eyed up the selections, she heard the woman two people ahead in the queue give her name to the barista. Karla.

Dana peeked around the back of the man in front of her and saw a person who looked vaguely like Peri's ex-wife, glancing around for somewhere to sit. The hairstyle was pretty extreme for someone her age. Without staring too closely, Dana saw that it was, indeed, Karla Sykes, who sat down at a table with her back to the wall.

When her turn came to order, Dana gave her name as Daisy. She didn't know why, but baristas seemed to have difficulty with her name and sometimes wrote it down as Dinah, Dino, or even Daley. She waited by the counter for the drink, not wanting to alert Karla to her presence. She watched Karla make a quick call. Her body language indicated she was meeting someone.

Dana settled in a seat by the window, her back to Karla's table. She pulled her notebook out of her bag and opened to a page at the back. She took a bite of her blueberry muffin. The blueberries counted as part of her five-a-day fruit and veg. Thinking how trim Peri was getting with all the walking, cycling and gardening, Dana felt a twinge of guilt. After consuming a load of calories, the only exercise she would be taking was the walk to the tube station. Perhaps she should take up swimming again. Although she wasn't too keen on the idea of using the gender-neutral changing rooms that had recently been adopted by their local pool.

A large man joined Karla. He seemed to favour the Steve Jobs style of clothing, black turtleneck and well worn jeans. On his larger frame, complete with beer belly, it didn't quite cut the image he was probably hoping for. Karla's boss, most likely. Peri had mentioned that casual wear was the norm for the IT company's employees.

She could only hear snatches of their quiet conversation. Annoying. The few words she did pick up sounded intriguing. Dana wrote it all in her notebook.

Bangkok, airport, mule, package, alias. going up north.

Karla left first, and the man went up to the counter and ordered a takeaway coffee. Dana gathered her things while he was at the counter and left quickly.

Once back home, Dana opened her iPad, relieved they had been able to fix it so quickly. She'd been worried about having to send it away, or worst case, buy a new one.

Sydney Devereaux showed up on the first page of the news app. The story was clearly a recent addition. Dana read through it, then looked at the notes she'd taken at Starbucks. The extreme haircut made sense, if Karla was worried about repercussions. The family wouldn't want to see Sydney languishing in a foreign jail.

If Karla wanted to hide, where would she go? Up north could be anywhere. There were the numerous liaisons, as evidenced by the phones they'd found in the house. Most of those women were in the southern part of the country, within easy reach of London. The only person Karla knew up north was probably Peri. Now that was worrying.

†

Karla opened her new laptop when the train left the station and entered her new username and password. Aldo had thought of everything. He'd even supplied her with a phone registered with her alias. The name he'd chosen made her smile. No one would connect her with Rhona Fitzgerald.

The wi-fi in the first-class carriage was a good strength. She opened the documents Aldo had preloaded for her immediate consideration. For the next two hours, she gave them her full attention. The train made its first stop at

Doncaster, and she was able to give him some of the answers he needed.

The next part of the journey was slower. The train stopped every ten minutes or so, at each of the main Yorkshire stations, before reaching Halifax. She browsed the news sites to check for any more info about Syd's arrest. There was nothing. Maybe the family had managed to suppress it, for now. Once her case went to trial it would be all over the media.

Any guilt Karla might have felt about switching the drugs to Syd's luggage had dissipated during the long flight from Bangkok. A surge of anger hit whenever she thought about how she'd been set up. Had any of her time with Syd been real? Or had Syd been faking it, making her believe they had a real connection, the chance of a proper relationship?

The sex had been great, but indulging her carnal desires had only caused her to lose everything. Peri hated her. Their home was gone. She didn't know she would miss that sense of security until it was no longer there. Maybe it wasn't too late to repair some of the damage with Peri. Their twenty years together had to count for something.

The rain beating down on the taxi barely registered. She took no notice of the scenery passing by the taxi's windows. The driver stopped the vehicle at the end of a muddy track and said it was as far as he could take her.

†

Peri was looking forward to a quiet day of editing a manuscript in the morning and reading the new book from one of her favourite authors in the afternoon. The forecasted rain had arrived early and was already beating on the windows.

The editing went well and by the time she stopped for lunch she was more than halfway through the document. She rewarded herself with a glass of red wine to accompany her tuna salad and granary toast. The rain eased off to a light drizzle.

Settling down with her book, she was engrossed in the story. A loud banging on the patio doors startled her.

The face peering through the glass looked familiar. Only when she moved to open the door did she see it was Karla.

Her soon-to-be ex-wife stumbled into the room, dripping wet and dragging an equally sodden suitcase.

"Sorry to startle you. I knocked at the front, but I guess you didn't hear me. Bloody taxi driver wouldn't bring me up that last bit of track. Worried about his undercarriage."

"What are you doing here?" Peri stared at the case and the backpack Karla slipped off her shoulders.

"I was hoping you could put me up for a few days." She held her hands up. "I know. I'm probably the last person you want here, but I need your help."

Peri sighed. "Well, you know where the bathroom is. I'll make some tea, and we'll talk about it."

When she came back with two mugs, Karla was looking drier and was settled on the sofa with her laptop open. Peri stumbled at the familiar sight, almost spilling the tea. She didn't notice the change of hairstyle until she was seated opposite. It would have made Karla look younger, if it weren't for the bags under her eyes.

"What have you done to your hair?"

"Part of my disguise."

"For fuck's sake, Karla. You haven't joined MI5, have you? What's with all the cloak and dagger?"

Karla turned the screen around, displaying a Sky News alert. Peri could only see the headline and the name that appeared in the caption.

"That was meant to be me."

Peri leant over and picked up the laptop. She clicked on the link and quickly read the rest of the story. Placing the device carefully back on the table between them, she looked at Karla. "So, why isn't it you sitting in a Thai jail?"

Karla gave her the same version she'd given Aldo.

"That's...well, that's plain evil."

"She was taking the chance that I wouldn't be caught. My guess is that she knew the authorities were on to her. She'd obviously been in and out of the country a few times, enough to flag up suspicion. From a conversation I overheard between her and one of her brothers, they planned to use me as a courier. Possibly from the very start of our affair."

"Shit, Karla."

"I know. I don't want to drag you into this."

"Well, you have now, by coming here."

"They don't know where you live."

"They could find out. Syd knows about me and about the divorce proceedings. That's on record."

"She doesn't know your surname."

"Oh, come off it, Karla. Even those of us not as IT adept as you can find anything about anyone online."

"But you don't have an online presence."

"My niece was able to find me easily enough by tracking you."

They sat in silence, drinking their tea. Peri observed Karla over the rim of her mug. Strangely, there was no fluttering in her stomach, or below. No emotional response to the woman she'd lived with and loved for twenty years, the woman who still featured in her dreams. This was the woman she'd shed so many tears over in the past few months, the woman who was still wearing her wedding ring. Peri had kept hers too, but it was in the drawer of her bedside table.

"I'm sorry, Karla. I can't let you stay here. I'll take you to one of the B&Bs in town."

"You don't mean that. Surely you can let me stay a few nights. You've always been there for me."

Peri slammed her empty mug down on the table. "Yes, I was. But where were you? Off shagging someone else, while I was playing the happy housewife. I don't owe you anything. And I don't want any part in this mess you're entangled in now." She marched into the kitchen, snatched her car keys from the bowl on the counter and her coat from the hook by the door. She stood at the entrance to the living room. "I'll take you there now. Let's go."

The drive was silent. Karla huddled against the passenger door, brooding, a familiar manifestation of displeasure when she didn't get her own way.

Peri stopped the car on the road opposite the pub that was closest to the town centre. "They have rooms. If they're full, they'll be able to recommend somewhere else."

"Thanks for nothing," Karla muttered, as she climbed out of the car and retrieved her belongings from the boot. She slammed the lid down and stormed across the road. A car rounding the corner barely missed her.

Peri pulled away before she could change her mind. She knew it was the right thing to do. Perhaps the time she'd spent with Raven was paying off, giving her the confidence to know what she wanted from life. This wasn't the time to let Karla take that away from her.

As if knowing she needed back up, there was a text message from Raven.

Still set for horse riding on Saturday?

Peri had agreed to give it a go, although she hadn't been on a horse in over fifty years. She hadn't liked it much then. She did look forward to spending time with Raven, whatever the activity. While stopped at the lights, she quickly texted back with a thumbs up and smiley emoji.

†

Dana watched the green fields and solar-panel farms flit by. The train hit top speed once past the London suburbs. Sharon had agreed Dana should go and make sure Peri was okay, although she wouldn't be able to drive up until Saturday morning. She was going to her parents' house for Shabbat. Although they didn't practice their religion formally, the family meals on Friday evenings were important to them.

Dana gave the taxi driver a generous tip. He'd grumbled a bit about driving up the narrow track but was kind enough not to make her walk. The heavy rain had started as soon as she got off the train in Halifax.

Peri's car wasn't there, but Dana didn't think she would have gone far in this weather. She tried the front door and was relieved to find it unlocked. Peri was getting used to country ways. She would never have left the house in London without locking up.

Letting herself in, she placed her overnight bag by the door. She slipped off her shoes and and switched the kettle

185

on. Coffee in hand, Dana wandered into the living room and stood by the patio doors. Peri had put a lot of work in. The garden looked amazing.

A meow reached her ears, and Jasper began rubbing himself against her legs. She reached down and scooped him up.

"Some guard cat you are, Jas. Has Mummy left you home alone?" She put her coffee mug down on the table and settled on the sofa. Jasper made himself at home on her lap. She stroked from top to tail and back again. The volume of his contented purring increased with each stroke.

When Peri returned a little while later, she was met by the peaceful scene of friend and cat blissed out together. Dana opened her eyes.

"Well, this is a lovely surprise. I didn't see your car outside though." Peri reached down to give her a half hug and peck on the cheek.

"No. I came by train. Sharon's driving up on Saturday. Hope that's okay."

"Of course. But to what do I owe this surprise visit? It's not my birthday."

"Um. Has Karla turned up?"

Peri stared at her. "Are you psychic? She did, but I've just dropped her off in town. She wanted to stay here. Can you believe it?"

"Unfortunately, yes I can."

Peri joined her on the sofa. "You know why she came?"

"Yes." Dana told her about the coffee shop meeting and guessing Karla's mystery destination would be here.

"I'm glad you've come. It did rattle me a bit seeing her again." Peri picked up Dana's mug. The barely touched coffee was now cold. "Do you fancy something stronger? I know I do."

"Sure. Whatever you're having. I'm easy."

"Ha. I know that." Peri chuckled and went into the kitchen before Dana could respond.

Jasper leapt off her lap and scampered after Peri, who carried on a conversation with the cat.

"It's good you have someone to talk to, even if it is just a feline who won't answer back," Dana called after her. She must have heard the tin being opened. "And I can see Jasper comes first in the pecking order. I suppose you're serving him first."

Period added ice to the shaker and measured pours from several bottles. "My special Manhattan mix." She returned to the living room bearing two tumblers more than half full. "I've made it fairly strong, but I'm not planning on driving anywhere else today."

"Perfect. I'll be ready to crash after this."

"I've got enough eggs for an omelette supper, but we'll need to get some supplies in tomorrow for the next few days." She took a sip of her drink. "Mm. That's good, if I do say so myself."

Dana sipped from her own glass and almost choked. "Fairly strong! This is lethal."

"Don't exaggerate. You're just a soft southern jessie, as they would say up here."

Jasper emerged from the kitchen and sat by the patio doors. The rain had stopped, and Peri got up to let him out. They watched him prowl across to the pond.

"He's fascinated by the frogs."

"Does he try to catch them?"

"No. He just sits and watches. Birds are another matter. He really thinks he has a chance of catching one."

Dana swirled the liquid around in her glass before taking another sip. "Did Karla tell you why she's hiding?"

Peri stared into her own glass before answering. "She's worried that Sydney's brothers might come after her. She was meant to be the one taking the drugs through the airport. But she discovered the package in her suitcase before leaving the hotel. She transferred it to Sydney's case while she was out of the room. So, it really depends on whether they realise she made the switch or think Syd was careless. Apparently their suitcases were almost identical. Karla had a rainbow ribbon tied around the handle of hers."

"What do you think she'll do now?"

"I've no idea, and I don't care. I left her at the pub. I guess she'll book a room for a night or two and then move on."

They were clearing up their supper dishes when Peri remembered her Saturday arrangement with Raven.

"Oh. I was going to go horse riding with a friend on Saturday, but I can cancel."

"Wait a minute. Hold the front page! You have a friend?"

"Don't sound so shocked."

"Well, come on. Who is she? Is this a date? I didn't know you even liked horses."

"Her name's Raven."

Dana lifted one eyebrow. "Seriously?"

"Raven Skybird."

"Now I know you're having me on."

"She's a performance poet. I saw her once at an Edinburgh fringe event."

"So how did you meet her here?"

"She's Hayley's mum. They all call her Nan."

"Right. And now you're dating her?"

Peri rolled her eyes. "I don't know the first thing about dating. That's such an American thing. Who *dates* at my age anyway? We're just friends."

Dana shook her head. "Methinks the lady doth protest…"

"Stop, okay. As well as being friends with their grandmother, I'm also an agony aunt for the two younger children. Bean needed advice with her periods. Poor kid's just started and in her first year at high school. And Rory doesn't know how or when to come out to his family. Those were just this week's problems. Oh, and before that, Adam went off to Europe with Rhiannon without telling anyone."

"I thought you came here for a quiet life."

"Really. It's hardly that. Not that I'm complaining. I do love it here."

Dana pulled her into a hug. "I'm really pleased that you do. Just hope Karla doesn't muck things up for you again."

"No fear. I won't let that happen."

A plaintive meow from floor level alerted them to Jasper's presence. He started to rub between Dana's ankles.

"I think he wants you to play with him."

"Hasn't he grown out of the string game?"

"He still likes that. Or hide and seek with a squeaky toy."

†

Karla settled into a corner seat near the fireplace. The pub certainly had an old-world charm. The first gin and tonic went down quickly. She ordered another at the bar and asked if there were any rooms available.

There were and they had one ready. She decided to forego the second drink and followed the manager up the stairs. He had raised an eyebrow when she said she would be paying cash. She quickly made up the excuse that she was waiting for a new card after the previous one had been compromised. She gave the ADIT office building as her address. That might have been a mistake, but it was out of her mouth before she could think of something else. Hesitation after the cash business might have flagged her up as some sort of criminal on the run. Which, in a way, she felt she was.

The room looked clean and comfortable. Left to herself, she opened her case and was relieved to see everything was dry. It was hardly worth hanging anything up, but she shook out the two shirts she'd brought and placed them on hangers in the closet. Everything else could stay in the case.

Karla expected she would only stay the one night. She didn't want to use up all her money with hotel costs. Aldo had included a wad of sterling banknotes with the laptop. Thoughtful of him, considering the mess she was landing him in. She had laundered the rest of the Devereaux dollars before leaving London. If they were marked in any way, she didn't want to leave a trail that could be followed.

Would her life ever get back to normal? What was normal? Nothing had been since she started the affair with Sydney.

The hot water from the shower felt heavenly against her skin. She hoped she hadn't caught a chill from the trek up to Peri's cottage. Another G&T would help see that off. Changing into the other pair of jeans and a fleecy top, she went back down to the bar and ordered a burger to go with the drink. Might as well load up on meat and carbs, just to be on the safe side.

Her feeling of contentment from the food and the alcohol didn't last long. Aldo's phone call put paid to that.

"The brothers have been to see me."

"Oh." Karla glanced around. The elderly couple at the next table were talking loudly to each other. "Did they threaten you?"

"Sure thing. Wanted to know where you were. I said I hadn't a clue. I'd fired you before you went to Thailand."

"Did they believe that?"

"I'm not sure. They looked like they might want to beat it out of me. Luckily, Fisbee and Luna turned up for the afternoon meeting and they left."

"Well that Loony Tunes Moonbeam would scare anyone off."

He laughed, and for once didn't tell her off for making fun of the American intern's name. "Are you okay?"

"Yeah. Warm and dry." She almost added that "Wet" Yorkshire lived up to its name but stopped herself in time. He didn't want to know her location. Best he didn't know in case the brothers returned to harass him.

"Well, stay safe. And thanks, by the way. The report you sent earlier was perfect."

"I aim to please. I'll have a look at that other project this evening."

"Good stuff. Ta for now."

She set her phone down on the table and looked out the window. The rain had stopped. A walk around the town might help clear her head and expend some of the calories she'd ingested.

Houses built at seemingly impossible angles dotted the steep hillsides of the valley. She sat in a café on the square and watched the passers-by through the window. Karla could see Peri fitting in this pretty town, with a mix of ramblers and cyclists. No one dressed formally. Karla was used to the black and white of London, with not too much variation in business wear. Rainbow colours dominated here, not just in the clothing, but also in hairstyles. Maybe she should get a purple or turquoise rinse.

She finished her coffee and returned to her room in the pub. Time to look at Aldo's other project. No good putting it off. After what she'd put him through, he deserved a quick turnaround.

CHAPTER TWENTY-THREE

Peri rubbed her backside. They began with a sedate walking pace that hadn't taxed her dormant riding skills. When they moved up to a trot, she remembered why she hadn't taken up riding as a hobby earlier in her life.

"That was grand." Raven dismounted from her horse with a practiced ease.

Handing the reins over to the stable hand, Peri offered a tentative smile. "Yes, it was…nice."

Raven laughed. "Sorry. I guess this won't be an experience you want to repeat. I thought, with you being a cyclist, it would be something you'd enjoy."

"It's a different motion. Anyway, I'm just glad I didn't disgrace myself by falling off."

"I don't think you were in any danger of that." Raven had followed behind Peri to make sure she was safe. Peri had caught her watching her buttocks, when she glanced back during the trot. It was a wonder Raven didn't fall off her horse from lack of concentration.

Peri drove them back from the stables and dropped Raven off at the farm before returning to Sheepfold Grange. Dana was playing with Jasper. A trail of his toys littered the floor.

"Good grief. It's like living with a toddler."

"Don't worry, Mum. We're packing up now. Sharon will be here in about twenty minutes."

"Great. That gives me time to wash off the horse smell."

"Didn't you enjoy the ride?" Dana smirked up at her. "With Raven?"

"Stop it." Peri tried for a stern look but failed. "I'm not sure I'll be taking up riding again. It was more painful than I remembered."

"You probably weren't doing it right. Takes practice."

"And what would you know? Have you ever been on a horse, city dweller?"

"As a matter of fact, I have. Well, it was a donkey on the beach at Blackpool when I was five."

Peri laughed and turned towards the stairs. "Is Sharon bringing lunch?" she called over her shoulder.

"Yes. She couldn't make it to Waitrose, but she picked up some of those hoisin duck wraps from M&S that you like."

"Fantastic! If she ever dumps you, I'll be first in line."

"Not a chance!" Dana shouted back, as Peri reached the landing.

†

Raven wasn't sure Peri's friends liked her. She walked down to the cottage for the pre-dinner drink Peri had suggested. Once the introductions were over, she had the feeling they were checking her out as a suitable potential lover. Their protectiveness was sweet, in a way, but kind of annoying too. Peri was old enough to make up her own mind. Raven had been taking it slowly, aware of the lingering emotional fallout from the disintegration of her marriage.

The restaurant was a new one to her. Peri explained she'd chosen it because there was less chance of running into Karla, if she was still in the area. On the way to the stables that morning, Peri had told her about her ex showing up and the reason for her sudden appearance at the cottage.

The more she learned about Peri's soon-to-be ex-wife, the more she disliked her. While some of her own relationships had ended badly, none of them compared to what Peri had been through.

If friendship was all that Peri was offering for now, she could wait. The time would come when Raven would know Peri was ready for more. Perhaps she could suggest they take a trip together somewhere. Christmas she would spend with the family, but that was over six weeks away. Plenty of time for romantic strolls along a beach on a crisp autumnal evening, stars and moon shining brightly, reflected by the sea.

When they reached the restaurant, Raven suspected Peri's friends were trying to keep them apart. Dana sat next to Peri, and Raven was left with the seat next to Sharon facing Dana. She gave herself a mental shrug. Probably for the best. She might have been tempted to make a not so subtle move under the table otherwise. She was sure Peri wasn't likely to be receptive to that kind of approach yet, certainly not in a public place.

The Londoners thawed out over the meal. Maybe it was the wine talking, but it certainly helped that she was able to say she'd read a few of Dana's books and enjoyed them. That was true. She wasn't just trying to boost the author's ego to enhance her chances with Peri.

"How do you deal with negative reviews, if you get any, that is?" As a performer, Raven was familiar with the way criticism could bring her down.

"I try not to take it personally. And sometimes, if they're not just being mean, there are valid points made. The ones that make me smile, though, are when they say there's not enough sex in the book. I mean, I'm not writing sex manuals. I'm telling a story. The clue is in the word romance."

Peri joined in. "Yes, I think there's the perception still that lesbian novels equate to porn, not just with straight men, but also our target audience."

By the time they left the restaurant, the atmosphere between the four of them was considerably jollier than when they'd arrived.

†

Through his blurred vision, Rory recognised the car that stopped in front of him. Relief washed through his battered body when a back door opened and his Nan jumped out.

"Rors. What's happened?"

He could only manage an incoherent croak.

"Never mind. Let's get you home."

There were two strange women in the car. One in the front with Peri and another in the back. Nan bundled him inside and fitted herself in, keeping an arm around his shoulders.

No one spoke, as Peri drove carefully up the lane, past Sheepfold Grange to the farmyard. She stopped outside the front of the house.

Nan supported his failing legs to help him out of the car and up to the front door.

†

"I take it that was Rory." Sharon poured wine for the three of them as they settled down for a postdinner drink. Jasper was already making himself at home on Dana's lap.

Peri accepted the full glass of red gratefully. She had stuck to drinking water at the restaurant, having offered to be the designated driver.

"Yes."

"Why would anyone attack him? He didn't smell like he'd been drinking." Sharon had shared the back seat with Rory and Nan.

"I know he doesn't do drugs, either." Peri sighed. "I also know he's not told anyone at school, or at home, about his sexuality. It took him long enough to confide in me."

"A homophobic attack? I thought they were more accepting of our kind around here."

"There are always a few who are less, shall we say, tolerant. I'm sure Raven will let me know what's happened. He didn't look in any condition to say much."

They heard the sound of a loud engine gunning it down the track.

"On the way to the hospital, I guess. I do hope he's all right. He's such a lovely boy."

197

They were on a second glass when her phone rang. Raven's name appeared on the screen.

"Hi. How is he? Do you know what happened?"

"Couldn't get much out of him. Martin and Hayley have taken him to A&E. I'm here with Bean, although she's asleep. From the little he did say, it would appear to be drug related. Seems some of Adam's mates have been on at him to continue supplying them in his brother's absence. He refused. I thought Martin was going to go ballistic. Seems he didn't know about Adam's dealing. As soon as Rory's up to it, he'll want the names of the cowardly little shits who did this."

"I'm so sorry."

"Don't be. I'm just glad we saw him. He might have been there all night otherwise, adding hypothermia to his injuries."

"Surely someone would have stopped."

"Not if they thought he was drunk or drugged up. Anyway, I'll keep you posted. Hayley promised to call from the hospital when he's been assessed."

"Thanks."

"Oh, and thanks for dinner. I enjoyed meeting your friends."

Peri ended the call. "Did you hear any of that?"

"No." Sharon and Dana were sitting close together on the sofa, both stroking a loudly purring Jasper.

She told them what Raven said about the attack.

"How much older would these boys be?" Dana asked.

"Five years."

"Wow. So they'll be a lot bigger and stronger than Rory. He's what, fourteen or fifteen?"

"Fifteen in January."

"I wouldn't like to be that age." Sharon sipped her drink, a thoughtful look on her face. "It makes my teenage years seem idyllic in comparison to what kids have to deal with now. Depression, self-harming, gender dysphoria. I suppose it existed, but we didn't have our lives exposed on a global scale through social media."

They talked for a bit longer, before Dana started yawning and Sharon suggested it was time for bed.

Peri washed up the glasses and texted Raven before heading upstairs herself. Raven still hadn't heard anything from the hospital. Saturday night in A&E was likely to be extremely busy. Peri lay awake, worried about Rory. Knowing that she couldn't do anything and that he was in the right place with his parents didn't help settle her thoughts. She fell asleep eventually, sometime in the early hours.

†

Raven shuffled around on the narrow bed, trying to get comfortable. She would have preferred to sleep in her motorhome but didn't want Bean to wake and find no one else in the house. She didn't often sleep in this room, while staying at the farm. The vehicle's fold out bed was far more comfortable and the small space heated up quickly.

She couldn't worry any more about Rory. There was nothing she could do. His parents were with him at the hospital. He was in the right place to have his injuries seen to. Instead, she let her mind wander to the earlier part of the day.

Peri hadn't taken to horse riding as well as Raven had hoped, but it had been a fun way to be with her. Thinking of ways to spend time with Peri took up much of her waking thoughts. She was glad that she'd been able to find some common ground with Peri's friends during the dinner. Dana, at least, talked enthusiastically about her writing and where ideas came from. She and Raven agreed that their best source material came from observing other people.

Raven recalled Hayley telling her that her school friends felt she was watching them all the time when they stayed over. As if Raven knew all their secrets just by looking at them. Dana was able to relate to that.

Peri had been quiet throughout the meal. Raven wasn't sure if it was because she wasn't drinking or if she was just tired from the day's activities. If the friends hadn't been there, if they hadn't found Rory by the side of the road... She would have what? She was sure they shared a mutual attraction, and it was getting harder not to try to gain some intimacy. A hug here and there, maybe venturing a kiss. Too soon and Peri might push her away. Raven didn't think she could handle that, even if it wasn't a permanent rejection.

Her phone pinged. Text message from Hayley.

They're keeping Rory overnight. We're staying with him.

Surely they didn't both need to stay. She could imagine Martin's simmering anger wouldn't have abated. She could see him pacing up and down a hospital corridor. But Hayley would be in bits and would want his support.

Sleep wasn't coming her way either. Eventually, she gave in and went down to the kitchen to make a cup of cocoa and grab a brownie. She knew where the special ones were stored. The combination of carbs and sugar might keep her awake longer, but at least she would feel happier about it.

CHAPTER TWENTY-FOUR

Raven was fiddling with the coffee pot when a sleepy-eyed Bean arrived in the kitchen.

"Where's Mum?"

"Good morning to you, too." Raven smiled at her granddaughter. "Now, what do you want for breakfast?"

Bean frowned at her. "Mum and Dad aren't here, are they? The truck's not in the yard."

Raven finished setting up the coffee machine and switched it on. She sat down at the table opposite Bean.

"They're at the hospital with Rory."

"Why? What's happened, Nan?"

Raven reached across the table and took one of her hands. "He got beaten up last night. He has some broken ribs and a head wound that needed stitching up. They just kept him in overnight to make sure he wasn't concussed. A bit battered, but he'll survive."

"Who did that to him?"

Raven carefully explained what she knew.

"That idiot. Smoking the stuff himself was bad enough, but selling it as well—" She burst into tears.

Raven quickly moved around the table and gathered the girl into her arms.

"Peri was right to be worried. Mum and Dad could go to prison."

"Well, it might be the push your dad needs to close things down." Raven stroked Bean's hair, storing away the information that Peri was concerned for her family. They sat like that until Bean's sobs subsided. "Listen, kiddo. How about you help me collect the eggs? Those birds frighten me."

Bean pushed away and wiped her eyes. "They do not."

"They do. Anyway, your mum will be shattered after staying up all night. So let's go get the eggs. We can have a family breakfast when they get home."

"Okay." Bean sniffed and wiped her nose on her sleeve.

Relieved that the girl was recovering from her distress, Raven didn't tell her to use a tissue.

By the time the other family members arrived home, Raven and Bean had everything ready for a full farmhouse breakfast. The bacon was sizzling in the pan, and the eggs were ready to be scrambled. The grilled tomatoes kept warm in the oven.

She tried to keep the shock in check when Rory came through the door. His face looked like he'd been through ten rounds with Mike Tyson. Livid stitches stood out against the pale skin above his left eye.

"What can we do?" Martin was wearing out the living room carpet with his pacing back and forth. "If we go to the police, we're turning ourselves in. It's a good thing Adam isn't here, or he'd be looking worse than Rory."

Raven let him vent. Despite his strong words, she knew he wouldn't lay a hand on Adam. Hayley had taken Rory up to his room after they'd eaten, then gone to bed herself. Martin was too wound up to join her.

"You know who they are then?"

"Yes. They've all been here and seemed like nice lads. They've even helped out during lambing season the last few years. Now their parents will blame us for getting them hooked on drugs."

"These boys, young men, are old enough to take responsibility for their actions."

"Yes, but they still live at home and act like kids. Adam probably started doing this when he was in high school. I just thought his appalling detention record was down to his lack of interest in anything academic."

"Perhaps it's time to stop growing the stuff."

"I have been thinking about it. The other option I've thought of is applying for a licence to produce CBD oil."

"You can't just stick to being a sheep farmer? You'd need some kind of lab set up to do that, wouldn't you?"

"I'm not getting any younger. Sheep farming is hard work and not that profitable. And now Adam's taken off, I don't know if he'll want to carry on when he comes back. If he comes back."

Raven patted his arm. "I'm sure he will. It's in his blood."

"I'm not so sure now. Seems he takes after my old man with his liking for the weed. Maybe he should join him in Amsterdam." He yawned.

"You should get some rest. I'll look in on Rory."

"Thanks." He pecked her on the cheek. "I'm glad you're here."

"I know I'm not the perfect grandmotherly figure, but I try my best."

He yawned again before nodding and leaving the room. She heard his heavy footsteps on the stairs. It was going to be a long day for all of them. She would see what Bean was up to. First she texted Peri to let her know Rory was back home.

†

Dana grinned at Sharon before placing all her tiles carefully on the board.

"That's not a word."

"It is." Dana quickly typed *qintars* into her phone's browser. "It's an Albanian coin."

"So it's a foreign word, which isn't allowed."

Dana sighed and removed the tiles. She put two letters down and started to mark her score.

"Qi? That's Chinese."

"It's accepted in the Scrabble dictionary."

"Doesn't mean I'm allowing it. I think the Scrabble dictionary is rubbish. There are no q words in the Oxford Dictionary that don't have a u after the q."

"Maybe in Jane Austen's time. This is the twenty-first century. The English language has evolved."

Sharon let out a heavy sigh. "All right. Just this once, you can have Qi."

"Hmph. You're only giving way because it doesn't score much."

Peri walked through from the kitchen. "Can I trust you two not to come to blows while I'm out?"

"Where are you going?" Dana looked up from the game.

"Just popping up to the farm to see Rory. I won't be long."

Sharon put some letters down. "Are you okay with having an early lunch? I thought we should set off before the heavy rain starts."

"Yes. No problem." Peri glanced down at the word Sharon had placed on the board. "I wouldn't accept that, Dana."

"Just go!" Sharon glared at her, and Peri took the hint.

†

Karla frowned when she saw the strange vehicle parked in front of the cottage. She hoped she hadn't hiked up there for nothing. Sometime during the night, she'd decided it was worth having another crack at Peri, appealing to her soft nature. She'd tell her she was running out of cash and couldn't afford to stay in rented accommodation. Not true, but Peri didn't have to know that.

No more news from Thailand that morning. She'd scoured every news source she could think of, but there was nothing about Syd. Probably not newsworthy. Just another foreigner caught smuggling drugs. During her searches, she came across an old story of a woman from Yorkshire who had received the death penalty. She was pardoned by the

Thai king but still had to serve twenty-five years in prison. She was allowed to return to a British prison after four years in a Thai jail, but because of the length of the sentence, she was kept in solitary confinement. A strong-minded woman to have survived that. Karla wondered how Syd would cope.

She lurked inside the open garage door. The small car looked like something Peri would choose to drive, and the Y on the licence plate indicated it was bought locally. The other car was more Karla's style. She thought the plates might be from a southern county. The visitors were probably that Dana and her partner, Sharon, the bitch lawyer. Karla certainly didn't want to run into them.

The front door opened, and she sank back into the shadows next to the vehicle. Peri came out, clutching a plastic bag. She walked past the garage and out the gate, then turned to go up the hill. Karla guessed she must be heading for the farm. She hoped Peri wouldn't be too long. The wind was getting up, and she hadn't thought to put an extra layer on.

†

Rory looked up from his book when the door to his room opened. He expected to see his mum or Nan. Seeing Peri come in was a surprise. He tried to sit up straighter in the bed but couldn't help wincing at the pain in his ribs. The painkillers had worn off a while ago. He hadn't taken any more that morning, as he didn't want to spend the day sleeping.

"Hi. You're looking better than the last time I saw you."

Rory grimaced. "I shouldn't think there's much improvement. Thank you for picking me up."

206

"Well, I wasn't going to leave you there." She sat in the chair by the bed and placed the bag she was carrying on his bedside table. "This is your manuscript. I've read it and made a few suggestions. Obviously it's up to you whether or not you'll agree with them. It's your story. I did enjoy reading it, and think you have a good chance of finding a publisher."

This time the pain didn't register as he managed to sit up properly. "Really? You liked it."

"Yes. I'm not just saying that. As you know, I read many manuscripts from first-time authors. Some of them require a lot of editing to make them more readable. I didn't have that problem with yours. The story flows well. I've just pointed out a few things that didn't make sense to me that you could expand on. Honestly, nothing major. You have a real talent for writing."

His mouth wouldn't quite stretch into a full-on smile. "Thank you so much."

"No rush on making the changes. When you're feeling better and have had a chance to work on it, we'll talk about approaching an agent."

Rory lay back on his pillows after Peri left. The idea that he could actually become a published author was the best tonic. He reached for the bag and hugged it to his chest, all pain forgotten.

†

Peri walked briskly down the hill. The wind had picked up, and dark clouds were hovering over the tops of the hills in the west. More rain coming soon. Sharon was right to want to head back to London now. Driving on the motorway in the rain wouldn't be much fun with the added spray from the lorries.

Rory's injuries would heal, the bruising would fade. She was glad she'd been able to bring a smile to his face, however pained his attempted grin had looked. Peri turned in at the gate, and a gust of wind almost lifted her off her feet. Head down, she didn't see the figure that stepped out from the garage until they nearly collided.

"Karla! What the—?"

"Can we go inside? It's freezing out here."

Peri noted the thin jacket Karla was wearing. Stylish for London but not practical for the countryside. "The answer is still no. You can't stay here."

"I'm running out of cash. I can't use my credit cards without leaving a trail."

The door of the cottage opened, and Dana came out carrying a case. "Thought I'd put this in the car before the rain starts." She stopped and gaped at Karla. "What are you doing here?"

"Nice to see you too." Karla started to cough, and Peri took pity on her.

"Come inside then, before we all freeze."

Peri put the kettle on and turned to face Karla. Dana came back in before she had a chance to say anything.

"So, what are you doing here? I thought Peri told you to stay away." Dana was in full attack mode.

"It's okay, Dana. Let's go into the living room."

Sharon came down the stairs with the briefcase that went everywhere with her, even when she wasn't working.

"Well, well. Look who's here. Do we need to get a restraining order?"

Karla opened her mouth to respond but ended up having a coughing fit.

"I'm sure that won't be necessary, Sharon. How long were you waiting out there?"

When Karla's coughing subsided, she said, "I saw you come out, but I didn't know who was in the house. I waited for you to come back."

"And just what do you hope to achieve by coming here?" Dana was still up for a full-on confrontation.

Peri wanted an answer too, but she didn't have the energy to release her pent-up anger.

†

Raven wasn't sure what she'd walked into. She'd only come to the cottage to deliver eggs and to thank Peri for cheering Rory up with whatever it was she'd said to him.

The woman she didn't know seemed to be the focus of the collective ire of the other three in the room. She didn't need an introduction to figure out that the stranger was Peri's ex.

All four heads turned towards her when she came into the living room.

"Hi. I brought your eggs, Peri."

Her words broke the spell, and Sharon spoke up. "Well, I think that's our cue to leave."

"You can't go yet. You haven't had lunch." Peri's words came out in a rush.

"We'll stop somewhere on the way. Come on, Karla. We'll drive you back to town."

"I can't stay there any longer."

"We'll discuss your options in the car." Sharon took Karla by the arm and propelled her out of the room.

Dana stopped long enough to give Peri a brief hug before following them. Peri stood rooted to the spot.

Raven walked to the front of the cottage and watched, as Sharon opened the rear door to the car and gestured forcefully for Karla to get in. She waited for them to drive away, then returned to the living room. Peri was staring out of the window. Did she want her to stay? Raven stood next to her and draped an arm tentatively around her shoulders.

CHAPTER TWENTY-FIVE

Rory walked slowly down the stairs. His strapped-up ribs weren't hurting with each step, an improvement from when he'd arrived home from the hospital.

He could smell freshly baked brownies. Mum didn't usually bake on Sundays, and she didn't bake any of the special ones when either he or Bean were at home. That distinctive smell hit his nostrils when he reached the bottom step.

Bean was filling the mixing bowl with water. She grinned at Rory before licking the remnants of the mixture off her fingers. He could see flecks of green in the batter that still clung to the sides of the bowl. What was his mother thinking?

The chair scraped across the floor, when he sat down at the table. His mum turned towards the noise, wiping her hands on her apron.

"There you are, sweetie. You do look much better."

"Who are these for? I thought you only baked them on Tuesdays and Thursdays."

"Well, I thought if the painkillers aren't working for you…"

He held up his hand. "I'm not Adam, and I don't want to get started. The pain's not so bad. Where's Dad?"

"Asleep."

"And Nan?"

"She's down at Peri's. Are you hungry, love?"

"Yes, I think I am."

"Scrambled eggs?"

He nodded. As well as being his favourite style of egg, it would be an easy meal to get into his bruised mouth.

†

"We can drop you at the station. Trains from there will take you wherever you want to go…Leeds, York, Manchester, Blackpool…." Dana eyed Karla's reaction in the rearview mirror. Their passenger was slumped in the back seat hugging her backpack.

"I don't know what to do."

"Well, I'm not sure why you're running away." Sharon turned to look at Karla. "You haven't done anything wrong. If these men come after you, go to the police."

"What good would that do? I'd probably be charged with wasting their time."

"It's make your mind up time, Karla. We're almost at Halifax." Dana braked to wait for the light to change.

"All right. I'll go back to London. If you don't mind giving me a lift."

Dana looked across at Sharon, who just shrugged. "We'll drop you at Boston Manor, if that's okay."

"Fine. Thanks."

When Dana looked back again, Karla had closed her eyes. By the time they reached the motorway, the woman was fast asleep.

"What did you think of Raven?" Dana kept her voice low, not wanting to wake Karla. "I hope Peri's not going to jump into a relationship just yet."

"None of our business. Anyway, it doesn't have to be a relationship, as such. I think it would be great if she were able to just take it as it comes, so to speak." She took her eyes off the road momentarily to grin at Dana.

"I suppose so. At least they're more compatible, age wise." She inclined her head towards the figure in the back seat.

Sharon placed a hand on Dana's thigh. "Don't worry. I have a good feeling about this one."

"Well, I'll take that as reassurance. You were certainly right with your first impression of bugalugs back there."

"I'm always right. Don't you forget it."

Dana read the number of miles to London on the motorway sign and sighed. Still a long way to go. She couldn't wait to get back to their home and relax into Sharon's loving arms. The thought of the long hot shower they could share brought a radiant smile to her face. She beamed at her partner. "Shall I risk breaking the speed limit?"

†

Peri stroked Jasper's head. It sounded like Raven was rooting around in the fridge. She would most likely find the ingredients for the sandwiches Peri had planned to make for lunch. They would need eating now with her visitors gone.

Raven brought two glasses of red wine through to the living room. She handed one to Peri. "Here. Make a start on this."

"I can't let you do all the work."

"Relax. It's no trouble."

Peri sighed and took a sip. "Okay. I don't have the energy to argue."

"Good. I'll be right back."

She reappeared, carrying a plate and paper towels. "Fine dining at its best." She placed the plate on the table and handed a paper towel to Peri. "No point in doing more clearing up than you have to. That's my motto."

"Thanks. I see you found the smoked salmon and cream cheese. I feel bad about letting the others go without giving them some food to take with them. Sharon brought these ingredients with her."

"Good taste."

Jasper put his front paws up on the table to sniff the sandwiches. Peri reached over to take one and nudged his head with her arm. "No, Jasper. It's not cat food."

"I don't think he agrees." Raven pulled a small piece of salmon from her sandwich and waved it. Jasper moved quickly and swallowed it in one gulp. He sat by her feet looking up for more.

"He's spoilt enough already. You shouldn't encourage him."

"Sorry. I have a soft spot for cats. Especially ginger ones."

The wine and the sandwiches didn't take long to consume. Peri didn't feel like talking, and Raven didn't seem bothered by the lack of conversation.

"Another glass?" she asked when both glasses were empty.

"No. I don't think so. Too much wine this early in the day isn't a good idea. For me, anyway. Please help yourself though."

Raven smiled and retreated to the kitchen with the plate and glasses. A few minutes later, she came back in carrying another plate.

"Dessert?"

Peri glanced at the square cut brownies on the plate.

"Fresh out of the oven. Hayley's specials."

They smelt enticing. Before she could stop herself, Peri reached out and took one. Breathing in the aroma, she was reminded of how they had made her feel. She took a bite and chewed slowly, letting the chocolate slide down her throat along with the herbal substance she knew would give her a lasting buzz.

"I'm not sure I should eat this after the wine."

"It's not a bad combination. As long as you don't have too much of either."

"You've done this before then.

"A few times. I'm not really into this stuff. But Hayley does make a good brownie."

The tension Peri had been holding in since seeing Karla suddenly drained away. She wasn't sure if it was the the extra ingredient in the brownie or Raven's presence that was making her feel happy. Everything in the room seemed more vibrant. The colours in the artwork above the fireplace looked like they were moving, blending in a dance.

A hand landed on her knee. Raven peered into her eyes. "Are you okay?"

Peri's smile stretched her face.

"Hm. I think you've had enough. Maybe you should lie down."

"Only if you'll lie down with me." Peri heard herself say the words as if from a distance.

Later, when she woke, Peri couldn't remember going up the stairs to her bedroom. She didn't remember inviting Raven to come with her. But Raven was there, stroking her hair. Soft, gentle movements. They were both fully clothed, lying on top of the duvet. Peri sighed, contented.

Raven watched Peri sleep. She'd been fighting the growing attraction since the first day. She was certain Peri felt the same. She knew she wanted more with this woman, but lying next to her was enough, for now.

CHAPTER TWENTY-SIX

Karla didn't remember much about the journey back to London. She'd slept most of the way and stayed in the car when they stopped to refuel and buy sandwiches at a motorway services. She didn't even know where they'd stopped. Sharon handed her a coffee and a cheese and tomato sandwich.

"I wasn't sure what you'd want. This seemed safe enough."

"Thanks."

She slept again after eating and only woke up when they left the motorway. As promised, they left her at Boston Manor station and drove off without a backward glance. Karla was sure they could have taken her further in to the city, but at least the Piccadilly tube line would take her close enough to the flat.

Karla approached the door to her flat cautiously. The lock didn't look to have been tampered with. It was a relief to get inside and find everything as she'd left it. Apparently, Syd's brothers hadn't found it yet. Not exactly a comforting thought.

The brief visit to Heron Ridge had made her mind up about one thing. She wasn't going to run away. Whatever their plans, if they did find her, she didn't think they'd risk long prison sentences for themselves by killing her.

The visit to the cottage had been a disastrous idea. Although she had only seen the other woman briefly, Karla was sure something was going on between her and Peri. The look she saw on Peri's face when the woman came into the room…She hadn't seen that smile in a very long time. She'd destroyed any chance of ever seeing it directed at her again.

Peri had succeeded in making the life in the country she'd dreamed of. Karla had achieved the exact opposite. Her only hope was that she would be able to keep her job. Everything else in her life was a total shambles.

After a shower and change of clothes, she felt strong enough to put on a load of washing and unpack a few of the boxes. A delivery of her favourite sushi meal from the nearby Japanese restaurant improved her mood further, and she went to bed feeling ready to face whatever the next day would bring.

†

218

"I haven't seen inside your mobile home," Peri said, as they walked through the farmyard. She stopped to look at the brightly coloured vehicle parked in front of the barn.

After waking from her nap, Raven had suggested they go up to the farm for dinner. Hayley always made more than enough for everyone, and she still hadn't adjusted her quantities from Adam's absence.

"Let me introduce you. This is Skyhaven." Raven opened the door at the side and gestured for Peri to go in first.

"Great name." Peri noted the orderly set up, which included a kitchenette complete with sink and stove. "It's so neat." She peeked into the bathroom with its small shower unit.

"No need to sound surprised. I like it uncluttered. When you live in a small space, it's good to know where everything is."

The driver and passenger seats were facing into the cabin, making it look like a comfortable living room. The woodland scene on the upholstery felt cosy. Peri sat on one of the side benches. "This is very comfortable. Where do you sleep, though?"

"That folds down to create a twin-sized bed. The futon and duvet are stored underneath."

"You don't feel scared, sleeping on your own in here?"

"Not if I'm on a campsite or caravan park. Sometimes, I'll stop for the night in a dark sky site to enjoy watching the constellations. Luckily, I've never had any trouble with unwanted visitors."

Peri tamped down the desire to ask about wanted visitors. How many women had shared this space with Raven? As if guessing where her thoughts had taken her, Raven sat down and stroked her arm.

"Look. I know it's early days for you. But I loved holding you while you slept. If you don't want anything more right now, that's fine. We don't need to have a full-on relationship. I'll be away for the best part of the year anyway. I would like more. I know it sounds crass, but maybe we can start slowly, just being friends with benefits."

Peri leaned in to rest her head on Raven's shoulder. "I enjoyed knowing you were there. Thanks for being patient with me. Maybe we can explore some of the friendly benefits after dinner."

She snuggled in when Raven shifted to put an arm around her shoulders, but Raven lifted her face to meet her own. The kiss was soft and inviting. A sensation she hadn't felt for a long time swept through her body.

Raven pulled back. "I think that's a good plan." Her tummy rumbled. "Well, something wants feeding first. We'd better get inside before Hayley sends out a search party."

†

The soft sounds of someone touch-typing on a keyboard reached her ears, as she stood in the space outside her pod. Karla swallowed. Had Aldo replaced her already? It was a thought that had nagged at her during the night. She could hardly blame him. She wasn't a candidate for employee of the month.

She'd reassured herself that her job was safe. He wouldn't have gone to the trouble of giving her the laptop with a new identity for her journey north. And she'd been able to give him the answers he needed on the two new projects he'd sent while she was away.

It was a relief to see the intern, Luna, sitting at her desk. Unless she'd had her work visa extended, Karla knew she was due to return to the States in a few weeks.

Luna looked up when she poked her head around the entrance. "Oh. Hi, Karla. We weren't expecting you today. I can find somewhere else to work."

"You're okay for now." Karla was surprised at how easily the words came out. "Is Aldo in?"

"Yeah."

"Right. Thanks." She walked past the vacant meeting pod. Fisbee was on the phone when she passed his, and he didn't see her. She felt like a ghost, wafting through walls.

Aldo was staring out the window but swivelled his chair around when he heard her approach. "Hey, Karla. I still can't get used to that hairstyle. Bored with country life already?"

"Yes. Definitely not for me." She sat on the seat by the desk. "I don't think I'm made for a life on the run either."

"Well, you might want to consider keeping a low profile for a while yet." He turned his desktop monitor around so she could see the screen. The BBC News headline stood out starkly on the white background.

"Fuck me! Twenty-five years! That was quick."

"Yeah. They don't mess about with drug crimes. Could have been a death sentence though. They're hot on that over there. Maybe her family's supposed connection with our royal family prevented that. The Devereaux clan might be able to talk that up on appeal, to ask the Thai king for a pardon. It's happened before."

"I know. I read about that case." Karla pulled out the SIM card that had fallen from a pocket when she'd gathered all her holiday clothes to put in the washing machine. "This could be my ticket to freedom."

"How so?"

"It's from Syd's phone. There will be messages between her and her brothers, and possibly emails if they're that thick. I think I'll feel less guilty if I know how far back in our relationship she'd planned on using me as a mule."

"What phone was it from?" Aldo opened a bottom drawer.

"A Samsung, fairly new model."

He rummaged around and came up with a device. "Try this one. Take it into the conference room. It's not exactly a Faraday cage but close enough in this building. Just don't activate anything new."

"Teach your granny." Karla took the phone from him and left before he could respond.

†

"I'd almost given up on you two," Hayley said, when they arrived in the kitchen. The rest of the family was already seated at the table.

"My fault," Peri said. "I asked Raven to show me inside Skyhaven." She took the seat next to Bean, while Raven seated herself opposite in the remaining empty chair.

Rory pushed the casserole dish across the table to her. There was still plenty of stew left. Peri helped herself before passing it to Raven. No one spoke for a while, with just the sounds of chewing and swallowing audible.

Martin scraped the last of the gravy off his plate and sat back with a satisfied sigh. "We've finally heard from Adam. He may be home soon."

"Oh." Peri looked up from her plate. "Where is he? Is Rhia with him?"

"Seems he only got as far as Amsterdam. They were staying with my dad, then Rhia went off with someone else she met in a bar. A woman. They were going to Berlin, then Prague to join up with some other people. You haven't heard from her, Peri?"

"No. I had hoped she would keep in touch. Is Adam okay?"

"Dad no doubt eased his pain with sharing a few spliffs. No, it seems he's more upset about what happened to Rory. One of his mates texted him. Sent pictures. I didn't have the heart to yell at him."

"What about those boys?" Raven asked. "Are you going to report them to the police?"

"No need. I've spoken to their parents."

"How will that help?" Peri was genuinely puzzled. "Won't they report you for growing the stuff?"

"We were all at school together." Martin smiled at her, as if that explained everything.

"They know what we do," Hayley added. "And they know we don't sell to kids."

"So, if everyone around here knows, why haven't you been banged up before now?" Peri looked at the Rushford family faces. None of them seemed concerned.

Martin shrugged. "I'm just a simple sheep farmer. That's all anyone will say, if asked. Of course, showing the parents the incriminating video one of the dimwits took and posted in the WhatsApp group did help. Adam's a member of the same group. They couldn't brush it off and say their son would never do anything like that. Bit of a shock for all of them." He grinned. "Anyway, what happened with your ex? I gather she turned up unexpectedly."

Raven jumped in before Peri could respond to the abrupt change of subject. "Peri's London friends took her away. I don't think she was enamoured of country living. Certainly wasn't dressed for it."

Hayley cleared the plates, while Raven and Martin commented on the weather and the possibility of another storm moving in overnight.

†

Rory glanced around the table. Now was the moment. If he didn't do it now, he might never find the courage. After Mum dished out the dessert, he cleared his throat.

"I have something to tell you." His voice came out in a strangled-sounding croak.

They all looked at him. He looked down at the table. This was more difficult than he'd thought it would be. Just a few words needed saying.

"What is it, Rory?" Nan's voice was gentle.

"I'm gay." He raised his head to see the reactions on their faces. Peri and his nan smiled. His parents were looking at each other. Bean was eating her apple pie with gusto, maybe hoping to have his if he'd lost his appetite.

"I thought you might be," Nan said calmly.

"Takes one to know one," Martin growled. He got up and stalked out of the room. The front door slammed.

Rory gulped. His mum reached across the table. "Don't worry. He'll come round."

"It's always hard for men to accept," Nan offered. "Especially with their own offspring. Maybe I should talk to him."

"No. I'll go." Rory got to his feet slowly.

He found his father standing by the gate to the first of the grazing fields. After a few minutes of silence, his dad spoke.

"Are you sure?"

"You mean, is this just a phase I'll grow out of?" Rory sighed. "Yes, I'm sure. I haven't told anyone at school, not even Trav. But I will. I'm sick of pretending to be something I'm not."

"Well, I always knew you weren't cut out to be a farmer, but I didn't expect this."

"So I'm a big disappointment to you in more ways than one." Rory tried, and failed, to keep the emotion out of his voice.

The silence lengthened. Rory could hear his heart beating. He was trying hard to hold back the tears, when his father's arm landed across his shoulders.

"I'm sorry. It was just a gut reaction. All we want for our children is for you to be happy. This, following on from the attack, was another shock." His fingers tightened their grip. "I'll always be here for you, Rory. Please don't ever feel you can't talk to me."

The tears did come then.

†

Rhia settled back in her seat with a satisfied sigh, as the train pulled out of Centraal Station. First stop Berlin for a few days, then on to Prague. She'd enjoyed Amsterdam, but Adam turned out to be a dead loss as a travelling companion. He was more interested in a tour of his granddad's favourite coffee shops than exploring historical aspects of the city. He'd fallen asleep during the canal cruise they took on the first day. He wasn't much good in bed either.

She smiled at her new companion in the seat opposite. They'd met while queuing to get into the Van Gogh museum. Vicky, a backpacker from Australia, was just as keen as she was to fit in as many of the sights the city had to offer as she could. She was pretty easy on the eyes too.

The train gathered speed, leaving the city behind, and Rhia felt a pang of guilt that she hadn't phoned Peri. The postcard was on its way though. She was enjoying the freedom of seeing new places and the fact no one in her circle of family and friends knew where she was. She just wanted to live in the moment.

CHAPTER TWENTY-SEVEN

Karla placed the phone on Aldo's desk.

"Did you find what you wanted?"

"More than I would have liked. She was intent on using me from the start. I didn't have a clue. I mean, I knew there weren't going to be wedding bells, but the relationship felt real. I never sensed that she was faking it."

Aldo held up a hand. "I don't need all the intimate details." He tapped the phone's screen. "So, we can use this as collateral should the Chuckle Brothers turn up again."

"Absolutely. Their attempt at a coded language is laughable."

"Good, I'll pop this in my safe for now. " He fished an envelope out of a drawer and wrote on it, before carefully removing the SIM card and placing it inside. "I have a proposal for you."

"Oh. Am I going to like it?"

"I think so. Is your Spanish still up to scratch?"

"I can get by." Occasional summer holidays spent with her mother meant she had been able to ace her Spanish language A-Level, but she hadn't used it much since.

"So, how would you like to spend a few months in Barcelona?"

"We got that contract?"

"Yes. We haven't all been sitting on our hands while you've been away. Well?"

Karla didn't let her dismay show. She grinned at him. "Perfect."

†

Peri walked down the lane to collect her mail. There was only one item, a postcard. The scene of bicycles chained to railings over a canal bridge was easily recognisable as Amsterdam. The short message just said *Moving on to Berlin.*

A postcard. How very retro. Peri would have expected her niece to communicate in a more modern way, text or email at least. Perhaps she thought her elderly aunt couldn't cope with that.

From the time Rhia had spent with her at the cottage, Peri had expected to hear more from her when she left on her travels. One postcard after two weeks was disappointing. Maybe she was expecting too much. She hadn't featured in the girl's life. Having solved the mystery of the skeleton in the family closet, Rhia was moving on.

Peri trudged back up the lane, postcard in hand. She recalled her own visit to Amsterdam with Karla. It was meant to be a sort of honeymoon after they got married. There hadn't been a ceremony. Just a visit to the registry office, forms filled in, and that was it. They didn't even need witnesses. The CP had been a formal affair. Peri had planned it to be the wedding she'd never thought she would ever have.

Amsterdam had been Karla's choice. She'd returned from a three-week stay in San Francisco and didn't want to fly anywhere. They'd travelled on the Eurostar. After wandering around the city and seeing the queues for the art museums and Anne Frank House, Karla was delighted to find the Bols museum. There were only two other couples going in.

Peri wasn't a gin drinker, but she found it interesting. Of course, Karla's main objective was to reach the bar at the end of the tour. Before going in you could choose your own mix for the drink. Peri asked if they could make something that tasted like whisky, and they did.

She stopped outside the cottage. That was the last time they'd been away together, she realised with a start. Five years ago. How had she let so much time go by and not known what was going on with Karla?

Although Dana and Sharon, and now Raven, told her she wasn't to blame, she couldn't help thinking that, in some ways, she was. She hadn't been paying attention. She should have made more of an effort. Was getting married a mistake that lured her into complacency?

Kissing Raven had awakened something, but it was buried deep. When they walked back to the cottage after dinner, Peri knew Raven wanted more. Although she'd thought she could handle it while they were snuggled up inside Skyhaven, the moment had passed. Raven must have sensed her mood when they reached the front door. She'd given Peri a quick peck on the cheek, then said goodnight and walked away.

Peri stood for a moment, torn between going inside and running after the woman. That moment passed, and she opened the door. Jasper greeted her with a plaintive meow.

"You've been fed, greedy guts."

He disagreed with a louder meow. She picked him up.

"Are you really hungry or have you just missed me?" Peri rolled her eyes at her own words. She *was* turning into a crazy cat lady.

She walked into the kitchen and wondered if Raven would think she was worth pursuing. It had only been one kiss. How long was she going to wait for Peri to make up her mind?

How long before *she* could let go of the past? Karla was history. There was no turning back.

†

Karla collapsed onto the hard sofa in the flat. She wished she'd brought the three-seater from the house. With everything else going on, it hadn't crossed her mind at the time. The sale went through without a hitch, and she'd been grateful for that. Now, it was just one of the many things she wished she could have held on to. Including Peri.

If she hadn't fallen into Syd's trap, she could still be married. Although she couldn't have delayed the move to the country indefinitely, it would still have been better than this limbo life she found herself in. She'd put on a brave act for

Aldo with his Barcelona offer. A few weeks there would have been okay but six months!

She still hadn't even unpacked properly, not that this flat was meant to be permanent. She would have to put anything she wasn't taking to Barcelona into storage. Aldo hadn't said so, but she suspected he would house someone else in the flat while she was away. If she came back for a break at Christmas, she would probably have to book into a hotel.

What would she be coming back to after the Spanish project was finalised? No home. A job that was increasingly populated with twenty-something hipsters who regarded her as an antiquated fossil, kept on by the boss out of misguided loyalty. She would still be on the lookout for some sort of payback from the Devereaux clan.

Peri was living her dream. Karla had fallen down a rabbit hole and was living a nightmare. She wasn't going to wake up relieved to find it was all down to an overindulgence of cheese the evening before. The if-only list continued to pile up in her mind, making an escape into sleep impossible. She pulled herself out of her torpor and got up to locate the box she'd placed in the bedroom closet. She had wavered whether or not to bring the phones with her. Lifting them out, she placed each bagged-up device on the bed. Who would be most receptive to a call? With only a moment's hesitation, her hand hovered over the one with Marli's name. A Swedish massage could help smooth away the anxiety pressing down on her chest. Too far away. Lacey in Brighton was a better option. Taking the device out of the bag, she switched it on. Battery life at sixty-five percent. Whoever had extracted the information as evidence for the divorce must have charged it up. With trembling fingers, she opened the phone app and made the call.

†

Raven pottered about in her van, as much as one could potter in a small space. Leaving Peri at her door the night before had been hard. She'd stopped at the gate, half-hoping to hear footsteps hurrying to catch her up. Instead, it was the sound of the front door opening and closing.

The evening was warm for the time of year, and she'd decided to sleep in the comfort of her pullout bed. She had just finished spreading the duvet across the top, when there was a tentative knock on the door.

Raven wondered if it might be Rory. She hadn't seen him all day. He had looked happier when he and Martin came back into the kitchen after his declaration, although it was clear he'd been crying. Tears of relief, perhaps. Bean was disappointed that he wanted his dessert then. Both he and Martin tucked in, appetites and spirits restored.

She opened the door and looked down on a smiling Peri, who was holding out a bottle of whisky.

"A nightcap?"

"Sure. Come on in." Raven took the bottle from her and stepped back, while Peri clambered in.

"I called at the house, and Hayley told me you were planning to sleep in here."

"Yes. The bed in their spare room isn't that comfortable." She closed the door and placed the bottle on the nearby counter. "Also means I'm not kept awake with the snoring coming from the master bedroom. I used to think it was only Martin, but Hayley's just as loud."

Peri looked around and finally sat on the edge of the bed. Raven took two tumblers out of the cupboard above her head, twisted the cap off the bottle, and poured a generous amount into each. "Ice or water?"

"Neither. No point in diluting a good Glenfiddich."

"Agreed." Raven handed one of the glasses to Peri. "Cheers!"

"Sláinte."

They clinked the glasses together and sipped. Raven enjoyed the sensation of the fiery liquid easing its way down her throat. She sat next to Peri and waited. She didn't have to wait long.

"Last night...I...I'm sorry. I chickened out on you." Peri's gaze wandered around the interior, finally settling on the glass in her hand. "I wanted to ask you to stay."

Raven placed her free hand on Peri's knee. "Don't worry about it. I do understand."

"I'm not sure I do."

"You were with one person for a long time. With the way it ended, I would expect you to be wary of starting up with anyone else."

"Everyone says it wasn't my fault, but I can't help thinking it was. Maybe I'm just a crap lover, and that's why Karla strayed."

Karla was an alley cat in Raven's opinion, but she kept that to herself. "I only have one kiss to go on, but it felt pretty good to me. Maybe we need to try it again, see where it leads." She took Peri's glass out of her hands and placed both glasses on the counter. "Are you willing to give it a go?"

Peri nodded.

The kiss was everything Raven had expected it would be. After exploring each other's mouths with their tongues, they moved apart briefly to get into a more comfortable position on the bed. Raven caressed already swollen breasts, leaning down to tentatively stroke each rising nipple with her tongue. Peri's quickening breaths spoke to her more seductively than any words could.

Raven's touch ignited something inside her, an explosion of a desire that had lain dormant for too long. Peri hadn't expected her body to respond the way it did. As Raven moved slowly down her torso, mapping out every inch with her tongue on the way, there was no ignoring the warmth spreading through her lower abdomen.

When she'd finished licking inside Peri's navel, Raven lifted her head. "Are you okay with this?"

Peri couldn't find her voice and simply nodded. She was ready for more, much more of whatever Raven could give her. Her toes curled in anticipation, as Raven placed a hand between her legs. A small cry escaped her mouth, as the fingers trailed through her curly mound and parted the lips, finding her wet and welcoming.

Raven's movements were slow and sure. Each stroke brought another spasm, bringing her ever closer to the release she didn't know she'd craved until that moment.

Peri was still shaking from the force of the orgasm, when Raven withdrew her fingers to replace them with her mouth. The swift, gentle strokes of her tongue brought Peri quickly to the edge again.

When Raven moved up her body to kiss her, Peri relished the taste of her own juices.

"Was that all right?"

"More than all right." Peri grinned at the face looming over her. "May I return the favour?"

"Only if you want to."

"Oh, I do." As they changed places, Peri thought how much easier this would be in her bed. She carefully positioned herself above Raven's supine form and began to map her own journey to the riches she knew lay in wait below.

†

"I warned you it wouldn't be a pretty sight." Rory held the phone at arm's length and aimed the camera at his face, so Travis could see the stitches and the bruising. Trav had texted him, wanting to know what had happened. Bethany's aunt was a nurse at the hospital and had seen him being wheeled into a ward for treatment.

"Hate to break it to you, mate, but it never is. Seriously, do you know the bastards who did it?"

"Yeah. Some of arsehole Adam's drugged-up buddies."

"That sucks. What you going to do about them?"

"My dad was all for giving them the same treatment, but Mum and Nan talked him down."

"Going to the cops?"

"No."

"Why not?"

"Better if I tell you in person." Rory planned to get the video of the attack off his dad's phone. He wanted to see it for himself and use it, if necessary, against his attackers.

"I'll come over after school tomorrow, if that's okay. I'm guessing you'll have a few days skiving at home."

"Sure." Rory took a deep breath. "There's something I do need to tell you, though."

"Oh."

235

"I'm gay."

"Hardly breaking news, shit-for-brains. I've known that since Year 5."

"You're kidding. And you still hung out with me?"

"Yeah. Why wouldn't I?"

Rory couldn't stop the grin spreading over his face in spite of the pain.

"But you do need to get over Mr Stevens."

"What?"

"That sickly puppy face isn't a good look. He probably thinks you're on something."

"Now you tell me!"

"If you want to start with someone your own age, the Phantom is hot for you."

"No way!"

Fenton Booth had been stuck with the nickname ever since Year 3, when the class read *The Phantom Tollbooth*. Fen was now six foot and being fought over to sign for several local rugby clubs. Now that Trav mentioned it, Rory had seen Fen in the library a few times after school. Not his natural habitat.

"Yeah way. Get your head out of a book now and again." Travis laughed. "Oops, Beth alert. See you tomoz." He signed off.

Second best to the girlfriend, but still his best mate. Rory grinned again.

He settled down under the duvet and the pain in his ribcage didn't feel so bad. First his dad's acceptance and now Trav. And Peri had offered to help find an agent. Rory Rushford, famous author. It had a ring to it. Life was good. He fell asleep, as his brain mulled over ways to approach a certain rugby player.

†

Peri woke with a raging thirst and wondered where she was. Slowly, she became aware of the naked body next to hers, along with memories of what their bodies had shared during the night. The woman lying beside her had awakened a sensuality that had lain dormant for a long time.

"What time is it?" she croaked. "Jasper will be wondering where I am."

Raven trailed a hand across her stomach. "I do my best to satisfy you, and the first thing you think of is your cat."

"Well yes, and the fact that my morning breath could knock out a herd of elephants."

"For that, I think you owe me breakfast. How about you go and look after Jasper's needs? I'll take care of my morning breath and bring the eggs."

"Slap!" Peri climbed off the bed and groped around for her clothes.

"Slap?"

"Sounds like a plan. Get with the lingo, old woman." Peri moved quickly, before Raven could land a slap on her bare bottom.

When she opened the door to the cottage, Jasper was sitting on the kitchen counter by the kettle. Peri could swear he was tapping a paw. His expression said, *What time do you call this?*

She fed and watered him, set up the coffee maker, and just had time for a quick shower before Raven arrived.

Her whole body was tingling with anticipation, as she moved around the kitchen. She set out the plates and cutlery, and poured juice. Raven arrived just as the coffee maker gurgled to a stop.

Peri pulled her into a tight embrace.

"Hey, don't crush the eggs." Raven pushed back to place the egg box on the table.

Peri grinned at her. "So, what do you want first? Breakfast or round two in my bed?"

"What have I done? Created a sex beast?"

"Are you complaining?"

"No, no. Switch off the coffee and lead the way."

Peri took her hand. "I like it that we're on the same page."

"Never in doubt."

Leading the way up to her bedroom, Peri knew this felt right. Raven had managed to bring her past the feelings of despair and inadequacy. Had she been such a bad lover? Raven clearly didn't think so. The way her body responded to Raven's touch, there was no doubt her awakened libido knew that age was no barrier to enjoying the attention of those loving caresses.

Jasper was asleep in the middle of the bed. Peri lifted him off and placed him gently outside the bedroom door before closing it on his startled face. "Sorry, bud. Playtime for the grown-ups."

She turned to face Raven and licked her lips. Country living had more than its fair share of attractions. Her dream was rapidly turning into a new reality.

ABOUT THE AUTHOR

JEN SILVER

After retiring from full time work, Jen thought she would spend her days playing golf, shooting arrows, reading, and enjoying quality time with her wife (not necessarily in that order). Instead, she started writing. Her debut novel, Starting Over, was published by Affinity Rainbow Publications in 2014. Jen now has ten published novels to her name, a number of short stories, and not as much time as she thought for other activities.

Book six, Running From Love, was shortlisted for a 2017 Diva Literary Award (Romance).

Book seven, Changing Perspectives, was a finalist for a 2018 Goldie Award (General Fiction).

Audio books include Changing Perspectives and Starting Over, both narrated by Nicola Victoria Vincent.

For the characters in Jen's stories, life definitely begins at forty, and older, as they continue to discover and enjoy their appetites for adventure and romance.

Take a look at Jen's blog: https://jenjsilver.com/ or find her Facebook: www.facebook.com/jenjsilver and Twitter: @jenjsilver

OTHER AFFINITY BOOKS

Before the Light by Samantha Hicks
One year after, her long-time partner Meredith's abduction, and their subsequent break-up, Kathleen Bowden-Scott's life is spiralling out of control. She meets Bethany Jones and despite an instant attraction Kathleen shies away. In this fast-paced, romantic suspense, lies are exposed and hearts unite as Kathleen and Beth fight for their future.

Wanted for Christmas by JM Dragon
Belle Farrow knew what she wanted for Christmas–work. She had little to offer but a minor degree in cookery and household management. Certainly not enough for a decent chef or housekeeper position. Then she saw an advert in the local newspaper. Wanted: Housekeeper/cook/nanny for the period of Christmas until the New Year. This is Christmas. Perhaps Santa reads the ad column too and pushes a little spirit of the season to that request.

Dreams in a Jar by JM Dragon
When you believe your life is a never-ending spiral of despair and the only personal joy you have is inside a novel,

would you grab a chance to hide away in the local bookstore and dream of adventures? Thea's life is about to embark on a journey she never envisioned when local bookstore owner, Marion, is taken ill. Her niece, Sheryl Appleby, takes over the reins and her presence provides Thea the courage to take a leap of faith. Can she embrace the butterfly effect, or are Thea's dreams bottled in a jar forever?

Pleasure Workers by Annette Mori
Alex Cortez is accomplished at two things, fixing broken equipment and pleasuring women. She is happily doing both at the Ranch in Nevada. Danna Nichols, newly widowed, feels lost and alone. When her good friend Lindy invites her to check out the newly established Trophy Wives Club, it awakens dormant feelings and desires. An instant attraction happens and the two form a bond under unlikely circumstances. Will the challenges of their social status tear them apart before they can enjoy the pleasures of their new love?

The Trophy Wives Club by Ali Spooner
What happens when under-appreciated professional women are offered their dream jobs? When one of Atlanta's elite businesswomen and wife of a prominent judge sets her sights on a goal, life begins to change for these women. Friendships and romance bloom in a unique fitness club on the outskirts of Atlanta, where more than a workout is offered.

Unknown Forces by Samantha Hicks
Jennifer Wilson spent the last seventeen years raising her younger sister Kelsey after a boating accident killed their parents. Riley hasn't had an easy life either and her

friendship with Kelsey is the only thing steadfast in her life. When tragedy and secrets emerge, Jennifer and Riley must learn to lean on each other. The growing attraction between them only complicates matters. When events conspire to keep them apart, will they trust the unknown forces that keep pushing them together, or hide from their feelings forever?

A Window to Love by Annette Mori
Two life events, two paths colliding, two souls destined to meet. Mandie Carter lives an uninspired life. No passion, no romance, and just when she thought things couldn't get worse, life throws her a curve. Gail Forrester is barely hanging on. Buried under mountains of debt, only her much in demand architectural designs keep her afloat. Now, they must find a way forward together through what life and destiny has in store for them. Only then can they hope to step into that window to love.

Free Spirit by Erica Lawson
Priory McAllister has fought off boardroom sharks, handled high-pressure jobs, and thought she'd seen it all. She found her dream home and couldn't wait to move in. Unknown to Priory, two ghosts...Rhee and a mischievous Dylan...have inhabited the house since 1935. They have no intention of leaving. Jacey Ryder, Priory's long-suffering secretary, gets to play referee between her boss and a bossy ghost, as each side try to lay claim to the house. What can she do when an unstoppable force (her boss), meets an immovable object (the ghost), besides hope for a peaceful solution? They are like two peas in a pod—two *angry, stubborn* peas in a pod.

Addicted to You by Erin O'Reilly
Elin Prescot's dream to be a top fashion designer is finally within her reach—then Marissa Banks enters her life. Snared by her first taste of passion, Elin is consumed by desire for more. Her life spirals out of control until she meets Doctor Aimee Sullivan, who understands all too well what Elin is going through. Can Elin let Aimee into her heart? Or will her addiction keep her enthralled with Marissa? This story explores first love, intense passion, manipulation of emotions, and the gentleness of real love and true romance.

At Last by JM Dragon
A perfume company in trouble, leading to a town in peril. Old Loves. Unrequited Loves. New passions. Can the reclusive Gene Desrosiers save her family company and the people she cares for, even though some are not aware of it yet? Will an ultimate sacrifice win the day, or will Grady end up a ghost town of unfulfilled lives? This love story will warm your heart.

Deuce by Jen Silver
When Jay Reid was in her twenties, she had it all. A professional tennis career, Charlotte, the love of her life and a new baby. Charlotte's research vessel, *RV Caspian*, was lost at sea, leaving Jay to raise their child alone. Rescued by a local fisherman, with no memory of her life before, she lives on the Faroe Islands as Katrin Nielsen. Seeing a beached seal one day triggers her memory. Twenty-three years is a long time. Is the love they once shared strong enough to be rekindled or have too many years passed, eroding all hope of a happy ever after?

Affinity
Rainbow Publications

eBooks, Print, Free eBooks

Visit our website for more publications available online.

www.affinityrainbowpublications.com

Published by Affinity Rainbow Publications
A Division of Affinity eBook Press NZ LTD
Canterbury, New Zealand

Registered Company 2517228

Printed in Great Britain
by Amazon

36299291R00145